Angels of Antipodes

ANGELS OF ANTIPODES

B. Francis Norman

Railroad Street Press

LIBRARY OF CONGRESS
CATALOGING-IN-PUBLICATION DATA

———————————————

Norman, B. Francis.
Angels of Antipodes / B. Francis Norman

ISBN 9781936711468

10 9 8 7 6 5 4 3 2 1

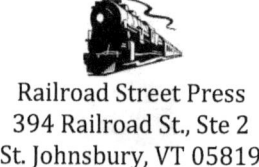

Railroad Street Press
394 Railroad St., Ste 2
St. Johnsbury, VT 05819

Dedication

To my mother and father, Beryl and Lyell.
They taught me a lot about family and history.
To my wife Karen who encouraged me to complete
this story.

Table of Contents

Prologue

What started as a search to return an heirloom, a World War One service certificate, led to discovering a series of poignant events for two related families in the early part of last century. They occurred during unprecedented social and technological change, upheavals from war, disease, and economic depression. This is a chronicling based on those true events in honour of the Bowen and Cabral families. Sadly, one of the family lines may no longer exist.

The true events themselves were previously dispersed in various records and newspapers, while some of the context used in this story is derived from accounts by earlier historians. These are cited at the end of this book. Nearly all persons named are real, with only a few exceptions (Anahera, Mike, Piripi, and Collin). Some persons, albeit only briefly mentioned, were named to honour their notable contributions to global events, and to show context for the period or places in which the Bowen and Cabral families lived (e.g., Kate Sheppard, Ernest Rutherford, William Ham, the Marquette Angels, and Michael Myers).

Some aspects of each main character (e.g., Alice, John, Rita, Jack and Audrey) are fictional, but still based in the true events. Having written this story about their real life experiences, I now wish I had known them personally; had lived in their time; that I could have expressed to them my condolences. Like for many families who encounter incredible challenges, their story need not be lost in the past.

EARTH

Palmerston North, New Zealand, Thursday, June 1, 1972

Gabriel might come only some days, but I could set my evening clock by him. When he first appeared, it was like he knew I had just lost my Caesar. He waltzed in then, as he does now, with aplomb and expectation of being fed. He pays no mind to hitting his head hard against my varicose veins until I place his food on the floor. While I eat my own oft-repeated dinner he sits nearby and preens his long white Persian coat. He seems unimpressed to ever again visit my one other room and bathroom. By the time the music and credits play at the end of 'Coronation Street', on the television each night, he jumps from my lap and heads for the door. He has at least one other home too. I can tell that from how he sometimes wears a collar and small medallion, which has his name on it. When I go out in the early morning to the front gate to get my milk, or later my mail, I sometimes see him striding down the footpath. He goes about undeterred by the bustle of kids going to or from school. I wonder what he thinks he is up to. I do look forward to his dropping in. He is my only dependable visitor. At first I missed the sounds of the trains when the main line was moved from the center of town. That was about seven years ago. They had sounded their horns as they travelled through the intersection at Terrace End, before passing the north end of my street and then heading out into farmland. On calm days I could sometimes hear them again in the distance to the east as they approached Ashhurst. I used to imagine myself on the trains, travelling to visit family and friends not often seen. I would see fields and farm animals, but close my eyes as we passed through tunnels in the gorge or cross bridges over deep ravines. There would be other passengers all excited too about the prospects of sunny days at the beach, picnics in the sand dunes, and daring to take a dip in the ocean. I do now, though, appreciate even more the quietness of my small rear flat. On warm days in spring and summer, and when my arthritic hands feel up to it, I tend my small garden plot of pansies, daphne, and violets. When my fuchsia shrub blooms, with its purple and pink teardrop flowers, I can picture again where it came from in my mother's garden in Wellington, and before that at my grandmother's in Carey's Bay. The happy noise of children playing outdoors is like music to me. Their sweet voices call out "Miss Audrey" to let me know they need me to retrieve a stray ball, often from among the lupine and rhododendrons at the back fence.

My office work has me out of the house only two half-days each week. I otherwise potter around my small flat, listen to the 'The Archers' serial daytime drama on the radio, and do a daily crossword. I enjoy short walks down to Memorial Park, which is on low terraced land in this otherwise quite flat city. My favorite thing to do is to take bread down to feed the ducks at the little lagoon. I will then sit there and read, sometimes my Reader's Digest magazine or a book from the library. Sometimes I write cards for Easter and Christmas. In some years I do receive one back from my cousin's wife in Dunedin.

Now that the weather is getting colder I stay more indoors. I have been re-organizing my scrap-books which I started when I was a little girl. One is on the Royal Family, especially Queen Elizabeth and her sister Princess Margaret, from when they were both young. I do not keep much on Prince Charles or his brothers, but I have a lot on Princess Anne and her interest in horse riding. I have another scrap-book on movie and song stars. I adore Shirley Temple, Vera-Ellen, Hayley Mills, and Julie Andrews too. I now have clippings on Malvina Major and Kiri Te Kawana. They have such wonderful voices.

My most precious scrap-book, though, is the one on my family. Mother gave it to me shortly before she passed on. She had taken great care in arranging the newspaper clippings, pressed flowers, and letters by my father. How hard it must have been for my mother and father to wait for news of each other when he was away at the first war. He never spoke of that time, at least when I was around. It has been a long while since I last could look at this family book. It starts with things about my father's mother, Alice, whom I never did meet. As I hold this book again it reminds me just how much I miss my mother and father, my grandmother Ellen too. Catching a glimpse of their smiling faces at my school and dance recitals has never left me after all these years; and Jack, my brother, what a rascal he was. It is still difficult to fathom how we lost him.

Christchurch, New Zealand, Saturday, September 2, 1893

Alice Bowen sat with her young toddler, John, on her lap while her four year old daughter, Emily, leaned against her side. They were surrounded by other women all exchanging news of people they knew in common and their best guesses at what was about to be announced. "What's this place mummy?" asked Emily. "Why are we here?"

Alice took a few seconds to prepare a response understandable for Emily. "This is a church hall, like the one we go to sometimes after our church. This is a meeting for women". Emily looked still bemused but satisfied her curiosity by seeing that indeed there were mostly women and only a few other children in the hall. Alice had come at the suggestion of her employer friend, Mrs. Tonks. She did not fully understand the purpose of the gathering herself. She imagined it might be to do with volunteering for church activities, and then wondered how she would find time to fit anything more into her daily life.

The excitement building up in the audience was palpable. Had Kate Sheppard herself been present at this hometown meeting the crowd would have quietened very quickly. They usually hung on every word she spoke. However, it took a few minutes for the speaker to gain sufficient quiet so as to make her announcement.

"Ah. My sisters! Ah, my sisters! Quiet please". She gently raised her hand to gesture a plea. "Thank you.

Thank you. My sisters quiet please. Ah, thank you! It gives me great pride, especially today, to make these remarks on behalf of Kate and other members of the Christchurch Women's Christian Temperance Union".

"My sisters and other supporters, it gives me such pleasure to again confirm how the passing of the Electoral Act by the Upper House and its ascent by Governor General Glasgow this very month finally acknowledges the right of women in New Zealand to vote. We are the first country to achieve this. Let us not forget those who began this journey in earnest before us. We have deep gratitude for Mary Ann Muller and Mary Colclough for their inspiration earlier here at home in New Zealand; For Lydia Becker, Helen Taylor, and John Stuart Mill, for their support from Great Britain; For Meri Mangakahia who with courage spoke at the Kotahitana parliament earlier this year. We should also acknowledge the support of Premier John Ballance who died just this past April. We are very grateful too for our sister Mary Leavitt's visit eight years ago now and the messages of support she brought from Frances Willard, Susan B. Anthony, and other American sisters of suffrage".

The audience erupted with such loud applause it momentarily startled young John. While Alice comforted John she wondered what was meant by suffrage, and how all those people from different countries knew of each other. She thought she would ask Mrs. Tonks next time she saw her. Perhaps she might now accept borrowing one of her books, instead of just dusting and returning them to the bookcase. The speaker continued. "Another notable achievement this year is that of Elizabeth Yates becoming the Mayor of Onehunga. She is the first woman to ever hold such an office in the whole of the British Empire". The crowd again erupted with applause.

"However, our work is not yet done. We do have detractors, such as Mr. Fish, who will continue to ply their booze money and ways to deter women from voting and from becoming members of Parliament. The General Election is this November, which is really only a matter of eight weeks away. We have to quickly organise and get the message to every woman everywhere that they need to get out and vote on November Twenty-eighth for the European electorates and December Twentieth for the Maori electorates".

Alice saw the excitement of all the other women, so she eagerly accepted a bunch of flyers from those being passed out to post around the city. She then placed John into his large perambulator and with help from another woman lifted it down the few steps and onto the footpath. It was big enough for Emily to sit at the opposite end, and when both children looked settled Alice pushed extra hard to get it underway. Once moving, its large wire spoked wheels with white tires looked impressive, and no cracks or mounds along the way in the path could deter its passage.

Once home, Alice had to firstly open her front door, lift and place Emily inside the front entry, and then maneuver the perambulator through the entry. She lifted young John and carried him to the kitchen and placed him on a rug where some toys were within reach for him.

Emily sat near him and played with a doll. Alice's husband, John, lowered the newspaper he was reading and asked, "So, how was your meeting"?

"It was interesting. There were some good speakers". Alice wondered whether she would try to vote, but then what difference would her vote make anyway.

"Good", was all John uttered and returned to reading in the paper about how the panic run on the Auckland Savings Bank had been calmed and was thought to have been started by rumor mongers in Sydney and Melbourne about rival Australian Banks. The notion of going to Australia to make a go of finding better paid work to improve his money situation had for a long time meandered around in John's mind. So news of the banks stabilizing again added justification to his growing desire to jump the 'ditch'. Doing it on his own, without Alice and the children, would make better sense so he could earn more money quickly; to be more available to travel to where ever the jobs were, so he thought.

Alice shoveled a small amount of coal into the stove fire and placed large saucepans with water to boil. She then began preparing potatoes and other vegetables at quantities more than her own family would need. It was her evening routine of making sufficient dinner for their boarders too. The newspaper was purchased for the boarders as well; otherwise John could not spare the change for his own paper to read.

"I met an interesting man today", said John as he lowered the newspaper again.

"I went to deliver some things to Canterbury College. I asked the man why some boxes were marked as being fragile".

"Uh ha", said Alice to show she was listening while still dicing vegetables.

"He is a scientist. His name is Rutherford; Came from Spring Grove, near Nelson. He said that some of the boxes contained materials for his experiments. He showed me around his workshop a bit. I didn't catch much of what he was saying, except something about physical activity even in hard objects. Anyway, he sounded smart. Not the sort of man I'd usually get to meet on my route".

"Uh ha", said Alice again. "Will you be speaking with Mr. Henry about paying his board on time this month? He will be away up to Wellington next week, and I would like his payment before he goes."

"Yes, I will try talking with him tonight. He's often not up by the time I head out in the morning".

Christchurch Supreme Court, Monday, August 17, 1896

"All rise. His Honor, Mr. Justice Denniston presiding", hailed the court bailiff who only briefly waited and then continued. "The charges read that Annie Taylor, of Harman Street, Addington, and Emma Watson, of Burke Street, Addington, on or about June Eighth, Eighteen Ninety Six, at Christchurch, did with intent to deprive Alice Bowen, a person having the lawful charge of Jane Watson, a child under the age of fourteen years, unlawfully take away such child and unlawfully detain such child".

"Mr. Donnelly, you may begin", said the justice with a hint of impatience and a Scottish accent.

"I call Mrs. Alice Bowen to the stand". Alice arose from her seat and tucked her dress and touched her hair anxiously as she made her way to the witness stand. She, as usual, was dressed modestly and remained unaware of how others found her soft fine features framed by demure auburn hair appealing. To her, looks from others always seemed condemning and not just on this day of court. Donnelly continued. "Mrs. Bowen, please tell the court where you live and what you offer as service in your home".

"I, ah, I live on Kilmore Street. My husband John works as a driver, and I rent out rooms to boarders".

"Was Mr. John Bruce Watson ever a boarder in your house, and if so when"?

"Yes. For about three months. That was two years ago".

"What arrangement did he request before he left your boarding house"?

"He asked me to take in and care for his daughter Jane".

"So you had taken care of this child Jane from age six until what happened in June this year. Tell the court what happened".

"I had sent Jane on an errand to a store just around the corner on Colombo Street. She had done this well a few times before and always returned with the correct items. She is a helpful little girl. But on the occasion back in June she did not return. I became scared for her, so I went to the Police Station to report her missing."

"And you had not given any person the authority to take the child"?

"No...No, I had not".

"Over the two years you cared for Jane, what sort of interest had Mr. Watson and her step-mother, Emma Watson, shown in the girl"?

"Mr. Watson would visit, about three to four times in a year. But Mrs Watson showed no interest. She never visited".

"Have you had any contact with Mr. Watson since June this year, and what has he indicated to you"?

"He has spoken with me twice and both times he said he thought I should continue caring for Jane. But he never brought her back".

As Donnelly returned to his seat Mr. Flesher, for the two defendants, quickly rose to cross examine Alice. "This arrangement with Mr. Watson, he paid you"?

"Yes, but he often missed payments. And funny thing is he paid me five shillings weekly over the past two months. He never said it was for arrears".

"Did the child Jane attend school"? , asked Flesher, with some cynicism and a glance to the jury as though they should pay closer attention.

"Yes, but....."

"What Mrs. Bowen? Had the child missed school while in your care"?

Some trembling returned to Alice's voice. "I was unwell......

"You were unwell, for how long"?

"Since February, I had no one else to take her to school".

"I see. Was the arrangement that she was to attend school"?

"Yes, of course. I did my best you know! She sometimes had no shoes and not enough clothes. I did read with her at home, and she learned things around my home".

"So she worked for you, took care of your own children did she"?

"No nothing like that. It was like I used to help my own mother when I was young. And I did take her back to school right after her own sister brought some clothes and shoes around for her".

Flesher stepped up the cynicism. "These errands that the child did so well at, was it to beg from other people"?

Alice felt a strong beating in her chest and flushed in her face. "I'm not well off you know. Not like some folks. I work hard running my house and have to put up with having strangers in my home as boarders. I don't like how they sometimes smell of pipe and beer when they come in, but I ...."

The justice interceded. "Mr. Flesher, unless you have a witness who can attest the child was sent about to beg then please desist in this line of questioning".

Alice wanted to answer more fully though and almost interrupted the justice. "I never sent her out to beg! Some ladies I've worked for, Mrs. Prins, Mrs. Burton, and Mrs. Tonks offered me clothes for her like they had done for my own children. If they didn't fit or they'd out grown them I sometimes sold them to the second hand store on Armagh Street".

Donnelly thought he might as well take advantage of the moment to also rebuke Flesher as he returned to his seat. "Mrs. Prins and others had given clothes not only to Mrs. Bowen but also to other women who worked for them. Mrs. Bowen did the best she could with limited means at her disposal". Donnelly continued, "I call to the stand Miss Ann Elizabeth Watson. Miss Watson, please tell the court your age and relationship to Jane".

"I am twenty one and I am the older sister to Jane".

"Thank you Miss Watson. Did you have occasion, and how recently, to visit Jane at Mrs. Bowen's home"?

"I would visit a few times each month. The last visit I made was on June sixth or seventh I believe".

"The court should please note that was just only a day or two before Annie Taylor and Emma Watson took the child without permission. Miss Watson, please tell the court of how you found Jane to be on the occasions of your visits. And were some of your visits without notice to Mrs. Bowen"?

"Yes, I would sometimes call around unexpected like, when I could get away from my work cleaning homes during the day and offices at night".

"And Jane...."?

"Oh, she seemed happy. I mean happy to see me and with being at Mrs. Bowen's. She had clothes and looked clean and not hungry. She never asked to go with me when I left, so I felt comfortable leaving her there".

"What is your view on what would be best for Jane"?

"Oh,... I ... wouldn't want to see her being taken care of by my stepmother or Miss Taylor. My stepmother had abandoned her".

Flesher stood and interceded, to which Donnelly gave way for him to proceed. "Miss Watson I think the issue here is the wishes of Mr. Watson, your father and Jane's father still".

"My father is kind, but not when he drinks... He drinks often".

Flesher hadn't anticipated such information so tried to change the subject. The justice said he would like Miss Watson to continue, to which Donnelly smirked.

"Since our mother died, about eight years ago, my father didn't take good care of us. My two brothers and I were sent from place to place and ended up in Burnham School".

"Go on....."

"My brother Fred, well...my father put him in the care of Mr. Isitt. I saw Fred once when he was in hospital. He told me he wasn't allowed to see me or our sisters".

Flesher decided to hand questioning back to Donnelly. "Would Margaret Malzard, please take the stand. Now Mrs. Malzard, please tell the court where you live "?

"I live on North Street".

"To what do you attest here today"?

"On June eighth I saw two ladies dragging a little girl from Kilmore Street around to Colombo Street where they hailed a cab at Haddrell's Hotel".

"Do you see those two ladies and the child here today in court? Could you point them out"? "May it be recorded that Mrs. Malzard pointed to each of Annie Taylor, Emma Watson, and the child Jane Watson. How was the child reacting"?

"She was crying and saying she wanted to return to her mother. She tried to pull away from the two women. They were telling her she wasn't well taken care of and that they were going to do so".

"How did the child seem otherwise"?

"She looked fed and dressed well enough".

Flesher took over questioning. "How does the child look to you today"?

"Much the same I think".

"You think? Does she appear to be just as well dressed and fed as to when you saw her on June eighth"?

"Yes".

"Thank you".

Donnelly stood and gave his summary. "It is perhaps obvious that Mr. Watson is not here in court today and you have heard nothing about whether he authorized Annie Taylor and Emma Watson to go collect his child Jane. The manner in which they took the child amounts to kidnapping. You heard from Mrs. Malzard that the child did not want to go with them and protested she wanted to return to her mother, who obviously she thinks is Mrs. Bowen. You heard from Jane's older sister and Mrs. Malzard that the child appeared to be well taken care of by Mrs. Bowen. Certainly we did not hear that Mr Watson had any complaints and continued to leave the child in Mrs. Bowen's care.

It seems that in the best interest of the child that she should be returned to Mrs. Bowen until such time Mr. Watson can demonstrate other proper arrangements for her".

Flesher arose to give his summary. "It is all quite simple really. Mrs. Emma Watson is the child's stepmother and can act on behalf of Mr. Watson to decide the care of the child. She had concerns that the child was not sufficiently cared for by Mrs. Bowen. Mrs. Watson had no criminal intent in taking the child and believes she has the right to be in charge of the child. The child really should be back with her own family".

It was a tense hour and a half late in the day waiting for the jury and justice to return. Alice again felt tightness in her chest and flushed in her face. Donnelly had tried to make small talk with her to help distract her, but had little success in getting more than a few short sentences from her. She couldn't bear to look over at Annie Taylor and Emma Watson who still had Jane by the hand, and she now had to withstand the last few seconds as the jury foreman read the verdict. "We find the defendant Annie Taylor not guilty". Alice's heart sunk and she felt as though all persons in the court were staring at her and that Jane had just been torn away from her again. She tried to contain her feelings but was so distressed she could not even hear the foreman read that they too had found Emma Watson "not guilty". Donnelly's telling her his regret and farewell, and the emptying of the court room, seemed only muddled noise to Alice as she remained frozen in disbelief. Thoughts of Jane being no longer a part of her and her family swirled around in her mind. She felt a piercing pain like someone had just punched her in her chest. The walk home and explanation to Emily and young John would be so very hard.

Christchurch, Saturday, May 4, 1907

Rain had stopped but the sun still remained shuttered behind grey clouds that stretched across the city and were stalled up against the Port Hills and Cashmere Hills. A few weeks earlier leaves already began looking weary in anticipation of further change to cooler air. Smoke from the many coal fires on each street whispered from rooftops to the ground, and in some places hung heavily between buildings. Smoke even lingered at the terminal cross atop the spire of the city center cathedral. Young John Bowen stood in Cathedral Square transfixed gazing up at the scaffolding that surrounded the spire. He swept his unruly brown hair away again from his eyes, so as to catch a better view. He was impressed by the two men he could see way up above who were servicing the copper sheathing of the spire. He wished again to be able to climb the steps inside the tower and look out over the city and the plateau that lay between the hills and the coast. Six years had passed, and he had shot up to be more than five feet already, since his last climb on his own at age ten. He frequently checked the church notice board for any announcement of the re-opening of the tower to the public. He was not afraid of heights and he remembered feeling more exhilarated than scared when the earth had shaken on the day the previous cathedral spire had crumbled.

"Hey John, are you coming?" said Emily. "Hello! Stop staring to the heavens, we have to go!" She then turned and strode away expecting that John was following her.

Emily was the instigator to get John and herself out of their house as much as she could, and this day was no exception. She had heard of a young writer's reading event involving many local schools to be held at the city library. Emily was an avid reader and so a frequent visitor to the library. She had grown accustomed over the past few years to taking herself and John places as their mother was more and more preoccupied with providing for the boarders in their home. Emily dreamed of being a journalist and reporting on interesting events and people. She did not let her dream fade despite the grind of finding adequate cleaning or retail work since leaving school.

As they made their way down to cross over Gloucester Street onto Cambridge Terrace, both John and then Emily suddenly halted. Other pedestrians had also stopped to watch a rarely seen vehicle that partially looked like a carriage but drove along noticeably quicker than the horse drawn carriages on the other side of the street. The vehicle had brass and wooden fixtures that contrasted with it being mostly dark green. The driver had his hands on a brass wheel and sat behind an extended front from which the sound of an engine could be heard. As the vehicle sped past them John and Emily could see a sign attached at the rear. It read "Fords at Dennison and Whyte Automobiles".

"Well here we are. Hurry John. I think it is about to start", said Emily as they arrived at the library on the corner with Hereford Street. Once inside John smirked with a knowing gaze at Emily as if to say "so now a long wait". Before them was a line of children writing in an attendance book and receiving an ink stamp each on top of their left hand.

Emily felt anxious at seeing the seating near to filling, but she was soon relieved when they found two vacant seats together and not even at the rear. She looked around and again admired the newness of the building. She remembered how the previous old wooden building had seemed much darker inside.

A tall thin woman, wearing a drab grey dress and jacket, stood at the podium up front. With keys dangling at the end of a long string around her neck and standing rigidly upright the woman looked as though she was on loan from a reform school. Some of the children sat anxiously wondering how she would address them but they were relieved when they heard her soft inflective voice.

"Good morning children and to you parents here today. We, the library activities committee, are very excited to host this wonderful opportunity to hear the voices of young writers of Christchurch and its surrounds. There were so many excellent entries that it made it very interesting but also challenging to select just a few for this morning's presentation. First up is Francis Percy with an excerpt from his short story 'The Man from Temuka'.

The tall woman guided the young Percy by his shoulders to stand down from the lectern as he could barely reach on tip toe to see over it. A few giggles whisked around the audience but soon stopped when another adult loudly 'ah hummed'. Percy began his reading with such a high pitch voice that some of the audience again let go giggles while others clasped hands over their mouths to avoid chattering. After getting a nod of approval from the tall woman Percy started again.

"On most days the cows and sheep would pay only interest in the grass. But that day, four years ago, was different. They stood lined along the fence. They all looked over to the next field which they had helped to graze only a few days before".

As Percy progressed in his reading his voice began to mellow and the audience paid better attention.

"At one end of the field there was what seemed to be a bicycle with a narrow roof attached above it. The sole person down there with the strange object could hardly be seen. He was stepping back and forth and after the start of a strange noise he quickly sat in on the object. The cows and sheep all glanced at each other as though each and every one of them did not know what to expect. The object began to shake and made a slow move up the field. As the noise got louder the object moved faster. When it got closer the animals looked surprised as it began to lift off the ground. They could see that the man sat upon a bicycle and frame that had three wheels. In front was a box from which all the noise came and so did smoke. In front of that was a spinning object".

The library audience had become fascinated with the story so far and so no one made a sound. Percy took a brief pause and then resumed.

"The object continued to bounce along, lifted slightly then fell to the ground again and again. The noise got louder and the man held on tightly as the object lifted again and remained off the ground, this time for longer. All the animals felt sure that the object would not clear the hedge at end of the field and they braced themselves for the collision. To their amazement the man and object lifted slightly higher, even higher, and cleared the hedge. The excitement was short lived as no sooner had the object flown over the hedge the spluttering noise ceased and the object suddenly dipped and fell to the dry river bed. The man managed to climb from the broken object and stood and waved to the animals as though to say he was alright and not injured".

Percy beamed with a broad smile of relief over finishing his reading and immediately looked to the tall woman for permission to leave center floor. The audience applauded with vigor and an exited chatter whirled around the room. The tall woman called for the audience to quieten and then announced the next reader.

"Our next presenter is Miss Edith Marsh who is going to read an excerpt from her short story 'The Seaside Sentry'. Edith was taller than Percy and so was prepared to use the lectern. However, at first she kept her gaze directed to the floor, or to the papers in front of her, and only sparingly looked up and out at the audience. She began with a tremor in her voice but only during the first sentence of her reading. Thereafter she maturely used her inflection to inject some theatrical effect.

"Soapy looking foam danced back and forth with the water lapping against the wall of large rocks. Debris of small sticks and larger driftwood floated in and out with some becoming captive in cracks. The gradual incoming tide eventually carried driftwood higher and over the line of rocks to the sand below the steep hill. With the slow tidal procession the driftwood frequently paused and then was carried further up the sand to be near other wood stranded there from higher tides. Up near the edge of the hill was a tree still in bloom with small white flowers with light sprinkling of purple spots. Although the tree stood tall it had over time been misshaped by past storms and broken branches. Its many remaining branches were full of tiny red fruit nestled between green leaves speckled with yellow".

The audience, but not so much John, remained attentive as Edith took a brief pause and then continued.

"The branches began to gently dance with a breeze that was gliding up from the shore. Far away waves were more easily seen by their white tops signaling a brisker wind was on its way in. Waves that crashed into shore were louder and larger. Nearly all the local birds had already flown in to find shelter in the many hiding places along the hill. Some were huddled behind the tree, but their feathers still fluttered with the wind. The leaves began to shake with such noise so as to send a signal to trees further back to be prepared. A lone bird was riding the wind back and forth out over the water, and then made a final bank and turn to fly with ease toward shore. With its massive out stretched wings it soared directly and then closely beside the tree. To every tree and creature on the hill this was the final signal to hold on tight, for the storm was about to make landfall".

Before the tall woman had thanked Edith and announced the next reader John had darted away from the audience. He had grown uneasy about having to sit and listen any further and so decided to spend time looking around the library. He counted on Emily coming to find him when she wanted to go too.

Christchurch Magistrate's Court, Tuesday, May 7, 1907

The court building on Armagh Street was a formidable looking structure of Oamaru limestone and gothic arches over its windows and doorways all reaching toward the high pitched roof. The large wooden doors moved easier than Alice had anticipated as she pushed on them to enter the building. She nervously looked around to ascertain which direction to head in, and was then relieved to see Mr. Hunt, her counsel, indicating to her to join him. After a snappy hello he then beckoned Alice to follow him into the court room. She could see that Frederick Hill was already present and in intense but quiet conversation with his counsel, Mr. Vincent. She thought Hill had glanced menacingly over at her so she immediately looked downward and swiftly turned into the pew Mr. Hunt had chosen for her.

The tension Alice felt only intensified when the bailiff announced," All rise. Mr. Bishop, Senior Magistrate presiding". The sound of the judge clearing his throat and the noise of people shuffling to reseat themselves seemed to reverberate for a long time.

The judge then spoke. "Mr. Hunt and Mr. Vincent please tell me if your parties have come to any agreement or are we to proceed"?

"To proceed", replied Hunt and Vincent nodded while with a bemused expression.

"I have Mrs. Alice Bowen to take the stand. Please state you name, age and place of residence", asked Hunt.

"My name is Alice Bowen, and" --.

Before she could finish Vincent interrupted "Your Honour". Vincent paused as though trying to steal the moment. "I think it important that the witness tell her legal name and not an assumed name".

Alice obligingly agreed with the judge's reiteration of the request. "My name is Alice, um, Alice Amelia Carlyle. I am forty one years old. I have gone by Alice Bowen after having lived nineteen years and had my two children by John Charles Bowen. He left me two years ago".

"How old are your children now"?

"Emily is nearly eighteen and John turned sixteen this March".

"Where do you live"?

"I live on Kilmore Street, but I need to move on account Mr. Hill....."

Vincent interrupted again "Your Honour, I object to the witness interjecting opinion when she should be answering questions straight-forwardly".

"Noted", said the judge and then turned to Alice, "As a witness you must answer the questions put to you and refrain from additional opinion".

Alice felt a resurgence of her anxiety, a flushed face, and wished she could just disappear from all the beady eyes in the courtroom that were staring at her.

Hunt could see her discomfort and asked a gentle question to ease her back into examination. "And your children continue to live with you"?

"Yes. They are both very good and mean so much to me". To which this time the judge looked bemused but let it go.

Hunt continued, "Please tell the court what happened to you on Sunday April Fourteenth"?

Alice began with a slight stammer but managed to say, "I had just left my church, the Spiritualist Church in the center of town. Frederick, Mr. Hill, followed me and grabbed my arm and threatened me".

"What did Mr. Hill say he would do to you"? As he asked the question Hunt glanced over at Hill as though to identify him again.

"He said he would do for me, cut my throat", said Alice with a shaken look.

"Why do you think he was threatening you"?

"He wanted me to give him some letters and papers that I had".

"And what were those letters and papers"?

"The letters were from him to me, telling me what he thought about me and his wanting to be with me".

"What about the papers"?

"It was a copy of his marriage license that I had found among papers he had thrown out".

"So how is it you know Mr. Hill"?

"He was one of the boarders who have stayed in my licensed house over the past ten years or so".

"Do you still operate your boarding house"?

"No I gave it up on account Mr. Hill wanted me too. He said he wanted to marry me".

"I see", said Hunt and then "Did Hill get these papers from you"?

"Not on the Sunday. He came up on me again the following Tuesday outside of Mrs. Bires's house. He pulled me around a bit, called me names, and grabbed the papers from my bag. I couldn't get them back from him".

"Were you injured at all"?

"Yes, he bruised my arms and I twisted my ankle with him pulling me about like he did", said Alice as she used her sleeve to dab a tear welling in her left eye.

"Over to you Mr. Vincent", said Hunt.

Vincent did not hesitate a second. "Mr. Hill will take the stand".

"Mr. Hill, please tell the court your name, age, occupation, and where you live now".

"My name is Fredrick Hill. I am forty four years of age. I am an advertising agent and I now live at the Riccarton Hotel".

"How do you know the informant, Alice Carlyle"? Vincent said with a tinge of emphasis on Alice's last name.

"I, yes, had boarded at her house a number of months".

"Had you ever kept company with Alice Carlyle"?

"No, we certainly had no relationship other than I paid for room and board".

"What can you report to the court with regard to the Sunday and Tuesday evenings referred to already"?

"On the Sunday it was her that followed me and spoke insults to me. I just ignored her and made on my way".

"What about on the Tuesday evening, outside Mrs. Bires's house"?

"It was her who came up upon me. She was aggressive from the start, called me a scoundrel and other names and she then tried to grab at my pockets. I never threatened her".

"Then what"?

"She continued to demand back letters she had written claiming I had breached her trust. I had not taken any such letters from her. I had taken back my marriage certificate and she continued to grab for it. Any bruising she got was of her own doing".

"Thank you Mr. Hill", said Vincent and continued, "Your Honour, if Mr. Hunt does not want to cross-examine, and so it appears he doesn't, I want to call Mrs. Anne Burgess and then Mrs. Claire Roberts".

"Mrs. Burgess, please tell the court your full name, age and where you live".

"My name is Anne Frances Burgess. I am fifty three years old and I have my house on Colombo Street".

"Please point to the parties you recognize as you having seen on the Tuesday evening in April outside of Mrs. Bires's house".

"Thank you. Please now report on what you observed".

"I saw both of them arguing and they were struggling over something one or the other had. I did not see who started it. They both seemed to be at it".

"How did it finish"?

"After some unpleasant remarks to each other they went their own ways".

"Thank you. You may stand down", to which Vincent turned to check that his next witness was being beckoned into the court.

"Please tell the court your full name, age and where you live".

"I am Claire Elizabeth Roberts. I am forty nine, well nearly fifty...next month. I live on Manchester Street".

"Please show the court by pointing to the two persons you saw on the Tuesday evening in April. Thank you. Now tell the court what you had observed".

"I was walking and talking with my friend Anne Burgess".

"Yes. Where were you"?

"Oh, we were on Worcester and came upon these two arguing".

"Alright, go ahead and describe what you saw".

"Well like I said they were arguing and pushing each other. Didn't last long and they both walked off in different directions".

"Did you see who might have started it or whether one or the other was being more physical"?

"No can't say who started it and it looked neither got the best over the other".

"Thank you Your Honour. That is it from me".

"Mr. Hunt, anything further from you"?

"No nothing further from me Your Honour".

"The witness can stand down. I can render a decision immediately. From the testimony heard here today the evidence of whether one party was the instigator or was the aggressor over the other is equivocal. Hence, I do not recommend this case for further hearing. The only instruction I have is for Mr. Hill to return the certificate to Mrs. Carlyle, considering he took it from her possession. He can simply request it back and she return it or he can obtain another copy. I suggest they do that via you gentleman, their respective counsel, or via mail".

"All rise", rallied the bailiff.

Alice froze and wanted to recede into the pew and not have to look around or be seen. She remained detached for as long as it took for Mr. Hunt to gather his papers, ignore Mr. Vincent's snide mutterings, and repeat her name to get her attention. "Alice. Alice. Come with me and we will find an office".

"I am sorry that it did not turn out as we hoped. Both Mrs. Burgess and Mrs. Roberts either did not see or remember enough. I need to be frank. Are you over Mr. Hill and do you feel he will from now on leave you be"?

"Yes, yes I should never have trusted him". Alice dropped her head and wiped away tears. She thought about being alone, unattractive, and hopeless about ever having a husband again. Her apparent vulnerability stirred some concern and then some momentary desire in Hunt, who then realized his awkwardness and quickly moved to finish their business.

"Good. I am pleased to hear that. Do take care and feel free to contact me should Hill confront you again".

WIND AND FIRE

Wellington, New Zealand, Thursday, October 28, 1915

The repeating slow approach and halting of horse's hooves and the clinking of milk cans being placed on door steps was a familiar morning call for neighborhoods like those in Berhampore. John had always been an early bird so his job as a milkman suited him well. He looked resplendent in his white uniform, cap and pin stripe apron. He was good at details and so had easily memorized the requirements for each of his many customers. Additional requests by any customers were easily recognizable by an extra small billy can or two with proper amount of coins. To John these were signs of his customers expecting visitors or their families growing in size. Over recent months though, some households had decreased their milk orders and John knew this was due to some people having already departed New Zealand for the war.

At the end of his run John led the horse and trailer back to the milk depot on Rintoul Street. The sign on the building read 'W. Crump Milk Deliveries, Partner In The Nutricia Milk Company 1911'. John hitched the horse and began unloading his empty cans and undelivered milk. His boss, Mr. Crump, walked up to him. "John, how about I give you a hand".

"Sure", said John with a broad smile and tapped Crump on his back. "Are you feeling alright? Don't usually see you out here before you've finished your cuppa".

"Don't you worry; this old guy will have to pick it up a bit again from now on! Show you younger guys how it's really done when you get back", said Crump with a wry smile.

The two men finished unloading the cans and John went to hang his apron before exiting the building. "Hey, John", said Crump. "You can count on taking a couple of days off before you go into service. I'll get Alan to cover your run".

John thanked Crump and quickly made off to walk over to Adelaide Road where he would jump on a tram coming from Island Bay on its way into the city center. The creaking of steel wheels grinding along steel tracks became louder as the tram came into sight. A faint spark or two could be seen from its pantographs reconnecting with the overhead electric line as it passed through the intersection. It hadn't quite made a stop while John boarded, handed his ticket to the conductor, and sprightly climbed to the upper deck. Other folks boarded only after it had paused. When it started off again the driver repeatedly rang the bells to alert other vehicles and pedestrians to move out of its path. From the upper deck John had a good vantage point to view the surrounding streets and sights. It was a sunny calm day and not surprising to John given the changeable Wellington weather and the torrential rain the night before. Within a short distance down Adelaide Road and over to his right he looked down at Athletic Park and recalled good memories of having attended among the thousand or so spectators at local and provincial rugby games. Although calm on this October day he remembered some games in which southerly winds played havoc with any kicking or line out ball.

Shortly after passing over Hall Street the tram paused again for more passenger exchange at the intersection atop of Riddiford Street. When the tram set off again John glanced down Riddiford Street and could see some of the buildings of Wellington Hospital just beyond pillar verandas at front of a grocery and a few other shops. He could not quite see his and his mother's house, just beyond and opposite the hospital. As the tram passed Hospital Road to his right John could see the large roof of the recently completed Government House among surrounding trees. As Adelaide Road finished the tram swung around to the left and continued around the northwest side of the Basin Reserve. John remembered attending there too on pleasant summer days to watch cricket. The tram then veered left onto Cambridge Terrace and paused for further passenger exchanges at two other streets. It paused for longer at Courtney Place before continuing on and left on to Wakefield Street where John got off at Cuba Street.

A wide banner with 'Enlistment Office' hung across the columned portico of the Town Hall. The national flag of the Union Jack and Southern Cross on blue background only lightly fluttered atop of the newish tower still awaiting its clock. John sprung up the front steps and entered to see a throng of activity in the foyer but an orderly arrangement of various stations in the main hall. At the entry to the hall he showed his call-up letter to a lance corporal working as the desk clerk who directed him to the bench seat waiting area. He smiled and gave a quick wave to each of two guys he recognized but were separately seated further ahead of him. Glancing around the room John could see that the first three stations each had a physician in a white coat carrying out examinations behind a trifold screen. The next three stations each had an interviewer whom John assumed were officers by the insignia on their uniforms. He realized one of the first things he would need to remember is all the various badges and their respective ranks.

To pass some time John picked up a copy of the prior day's Evening Post that had been left on the seats. He read about how a requiem mass for fallen soldiers had been held at St. Mary of the Angels, a Catholic church he had walked passed many times up on Boulcott Street. But he shrugged that story off to then read about how three Austrian aeroplanes had bombed Venice leaving casualties but no deaths. The Italians were indignant about the damage to some of their ancient buildings. Until then, John had not considered going in an aeroplane, let alone they being used in war. He tried to skip over other war reports but still on page seven he stopped to read how just two days before, fourteen girls and one man had lost their lives when trapped in a fire at a four-story factory in Pittsburg, USA. He felt it strange how such a tragedy had happened and not even in a war zone. While busy reading he had not noticed that most of the guys ahead of him had already been processed through the stations. Another corporal approached him to get his attention and handed him a slim cardboard file with New Zealand

Expeditionary Force on the front and unused pages inside, and then directed him to the now vacant second medical station.

"Good morning and what is your name"?

"John Bowen, sir".

"John, I am Dr. Shand. First thing I need you to do is to strip down to your underwear so I can examine you. While you are doing that you can tell me if you have had any serious illnesses or surgeries for any reason".

"No sir. I have had neither".

"How were you at school work"?

"I did alright, sir. Not top, but kept up with everyone else".

"Did you complete to at least Standard Four"?

"Yes sir".

As the doctor examined John's teeth, eyes and then inside his ears, he asked "Have you had any problems with hearing or vision"?

"No, can't say I have sir".

"Over on that easel you will see a chart. Recite the remaining letters on the same line beginning D, E".

"Yes sir F,P,O,T,E,C".

"Good. So John, judging by your white uniform you are either a baker, milkman or something like that"?

"Yes sir. I am a milkman. I work for W. Crump".

"Does that mean you carry full cans of milk? How many, do you think, you could carry at one time"?

"I could carry one in each hand if I had to, sir".

The doctor then used his stethoscope to listen at John's chest and then his back. "Take some deep breaths and let them out slowly. Good. Your spine is normal too and your feet have a good arch. If you can stand right here I will just check your height......

Five foot eight.....And your chest measures between thirty eight and thirty nine. Now on the scales....One hundred and fifty eight pounds. Good."

The doctor continued speaking as he wrote more things down, "Brown eyes, brown hair, and medium complexion. And John have you had any fits in your life at all"?

"No sir, I haven't".

The doctor then waited as John slipped his clothes back on and tied his shoes. "So, you look in good shape and have my clearance John".

"Thank you, sir".

"Good luck John. You can be proud that you will be serving your country. Your next stop is over there with the Lieutenant. Take this folder with you. Good man".

The Lieutenant looked up and smiled as he saw John walking over and indicated for him to sit on the opposite side of the small desk. "Good morning.....John", as he read off the folder John handed to him.

"Good morning, sir".

"I'm pleased to see Dr. Shand has given you medical clearance".

"Yes sir".

"Who should we list as your next of kin"?

"My mother, her name is Alice Welch. She did go by Bowen, due to my father, but she married last year to William Welch".

"Alright, ah, do you know her middle name"?

"Yes sir. It is Amelia".

"Thank you. And what is her current address"?

"Ninety Seven, Riddiford Street".

"So that is where you also have been living"?

"Yes, it is sir. We moved up here from Christchurch about four to five years ago on account of Mr. Welch".

"Your current job is as a driver. Does that mean you are also handy with fixing breakdowns"?

"Yes, I drive a milk truck and I can fix most anything mechanical, sir".

"John, have you had any run-ins with the police, or had problems with drinking"?

"No sir".

"What religion are you John"?

"I am Anglican, sir".

"Have you done any military service before"?

"Yes sir. I am in the Territorials".

"That is very good. I presume that means you have already been to Trentham Camp"?

"Yes. I've been there a few times, sir. I hope we are out of there before winter".

The lieutenant made a faint smirk. He recognized John was likely referring to the dampness that lingers in parts of the Hutt Valley for months at a time during winter. "You will be at Trentham again for a few months to prepare for your deployment overseas. Here, take this folder to that corporal over at that desk. You will soon receive a letter about the date you enter service, which will be in a month or two. Good luck to you John".

"Thank you, sir". John made his way to hand over his folder and then outside to catch a tram for a return trip home.

Trentham, New Zealand, Sunday, April 23, 1916

Propelling himself along under water was a sensation John enjoyed. The chatter of his fellow trainees who were still washing themselves became muffled and then silenced as he ducked under the surface again. He pushed off from the gravel bed for another short glide but heeded the unit corporal's earlier advice to avoid getting into deeper and faster water. As John surfaced again he stood and shook his head to expel water from his hair. He looked forward to the Wednesday and Sunday afternoon swims, albeit it was to make up for the lack of enough bathing facilities back at the army training camp. This day was cloudy compared to the bright sun the day before but the afternoon air felt to John to be in the same mid-sixties. That was until wind had begun to pick up a bit and was coming up the valley from the south. For a while John sat on the gravel shore of the river to dry off before putting on his khaki pants and shirt. He liked looking out and over to the western side of the river and to the Maymorn Ridge, its edge covered still with totaras, pungas and an occasional cabbage tree. He again silently congratulated himself for discerning where the Whakatikei tributary came out of the forested ridge and joined at a bend a little further north up the Hutt River.

John's daydreaming was short-lived however. The unit corporal extinguished his cigarette, announced the time was sixteen hundred, and called for the trainees to get in formation for the march back to camp. Their march back was usually a bit relaxed until they got beyond the farm land and closer to residential streets and the camp. While positioned upright and as though staring ahead, John and others were still tempted to glance to their left to watch a couple of horses on a training run on the race course that bordered the camp. There were some Saturday's that the camp personnel are given leave to attend the race meets. And a few of the race club buildings were still in use for isolating some trainees with sickness considered contagious. John was thankful he had not succumbed to any of the sickness that often spread quickly through the camp. He also thought about how he liked watching the mounted rifles brigades do their training maneuvers. He wondered how the mounted brigades were doing since they left with the Eleventh Reinforcements for Egypt on the first of the month.

"Bowen. John Bowen"? The night time duty corporal had stuck in his head into the barracks and called out.

"Yes sir, right here". John felt puzzled about what he was wanted for.

"Phone call for you, over at Captain Wright's office. Be quick"!

John hurried to straighten his uniform and made his way over to the office. He remembered to salute the Captain, who pointed for John to pick up the phone and for the corporal to leave. John had not used a candlestick phone before but quickly figured out to lift the stick to his face so to speak into the mouthpiece and hold the other piece to his ear.

"Hello. This is John".

"John. This is your mother. How are you doing out there"?

"Fine mum, how are you"? He was pleased to hear his mother's voice but John wondered why she had phoned.

"I am doing well. Things are much the same, but wish you were around here still".

"Is there anything wrong"? John asked, sensing his mother was being hesitant.

"Rita..." his mother started to say and John's mind immediately thought the worst for his girlfriend.

"What did you say"?

"It is Rita's father. He is not well at all. Rita went down to Port Chalmers on Friday. I have not heard anything since but thought you should call her to check on things".

"Did she say what was wrong with her father"?

"She thinks it might be heart failure. It came on suddenly".

"Oh, no. Poor Rita. It's a bit late now so I will phone her in the morning".

"Are you still going to be in the parade on Tuesday"?

"Yes. Can you still make it out to Petone"?

"Yes. Of course I will be there".

"It will be good to see you, mum".

"You too, dear. See you on Tuesday". Alice tried not to seem overly anxious about seeing John in just a few days.

John hung up the phone and the Captain re-entered his office.

"John, is everything alright"?

"No sir. My girlfriend's father has taken seriously ill. I want to call her early tomorrow, if that is okay".

"I will instruct my corporal to advise your unit that you can be excused anytime tomorrow to come make your phone call". The Captain did not say he suspected it might be the last time John would get to talk with his girlfriend.

"Thank you sir", as he saluted and left the office.

John had tossed and turned throughout the night. It had been many weeks since he had not felt ready to arise right on morning call. His worry for Rita was still on his mind so he mechanically went through the motions of dressing, going to the toilet, and reporting outside in front of his barracks. He did not even register that the air felt cooler than the day before and that a light rain had started. Once he was dismissed he meandered into the mess hall for breakfast without thinking much about what he ate. He checked with his unit corporal and then headed directly over to the captain's office.

When the office corporal announced that he had successfully put the call through to Carey's Bay, Port Chalmers he advised John he could pick up the phone.

"Rita, Rita honey. Are you there"?

"John ..." and Rita then began sobbing.

"Rita dear, how is your father"?

"He is gone! My mother is distraught. I don't know what to do".

"Gone! Rita, what happened"? John frantically looked around the office as the reality of the news sank in.

"It was his heart. I can't believe it. My father…he was fine".

"Oh my gosh! Rita honey. I should be there with you. Your poor mother".

"Yes, yes".

"Are John and Anthony okay"?

"We are all just numb".

"Rita, I am so sorry I can't be there. This damn war"! John struggled to think of ways to get down to Rita, all the while knowing it was not possible.

"No, no don't worry. We all know you cannot come down here. I'm sorry I won't get to see you tomorrow".

"I will try and phone again soon. Or have my mother call me if you need, will you Honey"?

"I will John. I love you. Take care".

"Love you too Honey. I can't wait to see you again".

Hearing Rita's voice for the first time in a long while resonated with John for the remainder of the day. He went about his training exercises and chores still in a slight trance. He felt sad for Rita. His longing for her took over his mind from attending as usual to his training, and he felt disappointed by not being able to see her as planned for the following day. By evening time he realized he needed to organize his dress uniform and remember his instructions for the train ride and parade the next day. Still feeling lonely for Rita he was glad to sink into his bed and for curfew so his bunk-mates would quieten down.

Petone, New Zealand, First ANZAC Anniversary, Tuesday, April 25, 1916

Sunshine was back and many at the camp were busy preparing for the train ride and the ceremony. The camp band practiced its music, at both standing still and marching. John felt some pride that it was his unit that was chosen to accompany the forty-strong band, to assist carrying equipment and to be part of the honour guard. It was a timely distraction from thinking about the forthcoming departure for the war. Those going to the ceremony assembled on the camp parade ground and then marched down to the Trentham train station on Racecourse Road. Waiting at the station was a Price B Class steam locomotive and in short time all the band and accompanying soldiers and officers were aboard the three wooden clad passenger carriages for the thirty minute non-stop ride to Petone.

Steam was already billowing from the chimney with good pressure by the time the train had passed by the Silverstream Bridge Station. Once through the narrowing of the valley between Upper Hutt and Lower Hutt the train built further speed and followed the lower edge of the western hills. It began to decelerate when at Melling and was at a slow crawl when the driver leaned from his window to check a semaphore signal and ease the train through the points leading to a siding at Petone Station.

When John and his fellow soldiers disembarked the train they first noticed a new large flag pole, absent of any flags. As they approached the station buildings they admired the additional platform that had been erected for the event. It was decorated with numerous small flags, ferns and potted plants. A solitary Union Jack, with its symmetric and saltire crosses, flew on another pole. Two huge banners of military theme framed the raised bleachers on which numerous school children stood ready to sing. Girls wore white or cream bonnets and boys had dark caps. Many more children stood lower on the actual station platform too. The band and John's unit halted and kept formation horizontal with the raised platform and then in unison turned to stand at attention facing the podium. Behind them were hundreds of general public, among whom John had not yet spotted his mother.

The ministerial officials arrived and started proceedings right at the planned time of three thirty. The master of ceremonies stood forth and made the opening remarks.

"I have great pride as mayor that this occasion takes place here at Petone. I congratulate the railway-men of the district for their public-spirited effort in making all the arrangements and this fine venue for this special day. It is exceedingly fitting that this special function of unfurling a flag received from their fellow railway-men of New South Wales, and our own New Zealand flag, takes place on this commemoration of Anzac Day. It is twelve months since Australians and New Zealanders first fought together at Gallipoli". The crowd erupted with applause. "On this same day at Hornsby, Sydney, a similar function of unfurling our respective flags is happening as we stand here now". The audience applauded again. "It is with pleasure that I now hand over to Sergeant-Major Fox of the Trentham Camp Band".

The band played a selection of short military tunes and just as Fox brought his baton down on the last tune the mayor rose again to welcome the next speaker.

"It is my privilege to ask our Prime Minister the Right Honorable William Massey to next address this special occasion".

"Thank you Mayor McEwan, and the people of Petone. I firstly want to acknowledge the organisers of this commemoration and those here in attendance today. We gather here together like so many around the country and Australia to honour our service men and women. I, too, feel honored by you having asked me to unfurl the flag presented to the Petone men from the railway-men of the sister state of New South Wales. It is indeed a splendid idea for the exchange of flags to occur on this very first anniversary of Anzac. It so bodes well for promoting the feeling of kinship and friendship that we all desire, for love of country, love of Empire, and a feeling of confidence between this country and Australia. It was twelve months ago today that the fighting men of Australia and New Zealand fought shoulder to shoulder against such over-whelming odds. They had to pass through such a storm of shot and shell such as no British soldiers had ever experienced. They were weighed in the balance and were not found wanting. They won out. Let me paraphrase a prominent British statesmen, 'I love England, I love Scotland, I love Ireland; I love their people. But I take my hat off in awe and veneration to that branch of the British stock that gave us the Australasians'. There is not the slightest doubt that the Anzacs have done credit for all of us here today and for the whole of this Dominion". The Petone assemblage erupted again with applause. Massey continued.

"I say to you today that the New South Wales flag and our New Zealand Flag are both British flags, and stand for one people, one language, one destiny, and one ideal. And the one ideal of these two great people today and for all time is the uplifting of humanity".

The crowd loudly applauded and cheered. Then the choir master briskly took center stage and with fervent downward wave of his arm set the children to sing 'Rule Britannia'. The audience sung along and waved hundreds of miniature Union Jacks while Prime Minister Massey unfurled the red ensign from New South Wales. He was assisted by one railway-man and one soldier to hoist it up the flag pole. The soldiers present all saluted.

The mayor rose again to announce the next speaker. "Thank you Mr. Foster, the children of Petone High School and district, and of Korokoro and convent schools. Your voices give such honor for this occasion. It is now also my privilege to welcome our next speaker the honorable Sir Joseph Ward".

"Thank you Mr. Mayor, and all the fine people of Petone. It is indeed superb that among you are the railway-men of the largest railways workshop center who have responded with such spirit to the offer from the New South Wales railway-men for this exchange of flags. It is tremendous how this Petone workshop has produced wagons, carts, and machine guns for the war and is capable of producing more for our forces at the front lines". The crowd cheered and applauded. "It is thus fitting that the public should assemble here at this center for this unique ceremony; unique because, as far as I am aware, no other such ceremony has been held in any other part of the British Dominions. And if not for the war, this exchange of flags might not have occurred and it resembles how it has brought the peoples of both Australia and New Zealand much closer together". As he said it, Ward reflected on his earlier private conversation and agreement with Massey, usually his political rival, about some lessons of Gallipoli and seeking military command over New Zealand forces independent from the British hierarchy. Ward then continued. "I should bring to all of your attention, and for all of us to take pride in that of the twelve thousand railway-men of New Zealand, a third of these have joined the military mission. Of these, two thousand have enlisted or have already made their way to the fronts. And of this number, as far as I can ascertain, seventy five have laid down their lives for King and country". The audience let out a collective sigh and Ward used the pause to build more bluster to deliver a resounding finish. "We are not yet in sight of the end of this war, but we are in sight of one indisputable part. It is the solid determination of the British Empire, including these railway-men and other fine soldiers of New Zealand, which will see us through to a successful conclusion". Ward then stepped forward and he too was assisted by a railway-men and a soldier to unfurl and hoist the New Zealand national flag.

The mayor led the crowd in three cheers and then announced a final speaker. "I have great pleasure in introducing to you a venerable gentleman here today representing the railway-men of New South Wales, Mr. Stone, Junior".

Mr. Stone stood, approached the podium and began speaking with a distinguishable Australian accent. "On behalf of my fellow railway-men of New South Wales I would like to acknowledge the sentiment of all the prior speakers, in particular that of our brotherhood during this time of war. I bring to you today the well wishes of my fellow railway-men. It is fitting that a ceremony such as this is happening also at Hornsby, our home base railway center. We too feel the same, that together we shall see this war through to victory. Thank you."

The crowd applauded loudly and with the band underway again all present fell into singing the national anthem of New Zealand. All the soldiers present, those from the camp and veterans in the crowd, saluted. Once the anthem was over Sergeant-Major Fox brought the band and honour guard about turn and marched them a short distance from the platform. He announced to them that they could spend twenty minutes with any family and friends present, and then return to the train.

John had difficulty identifying his mother among the many other women who wore similar muted coloured long coats and hats. Alice had no problem seeing John and so when she called out it was her voice he at first recognized. "There you are! I could not find you among this crowd", he said.

"Oh, John. I finally get to see you", said Alice as she reached out to hug John. "You look so dapper in your uniform", she said as they broke their embrace.

"So how was the ride out from Wellington"?

"Not too bad. Just about everyone was making their way here, so everyone was pleasant".

"What did you think of the commemoration"? John tried to keep up the pretense of things being normal.

"I liked the children's choir and the band, but there could have been fewer speeches".

"Yes, it felt like they took a long time".

"You did get to talk with Rita"?

"Yes. I talked with her yesterday. Her father had just passed".

"Oh, I feel so sad for Rita, and her mother too; so soon after losing their little Hilda. It all happened so fast".

"Yes, he was at home. There was nothing more they could do".

"I am going to write to her when I get home". Alice was already considering what to write.

"I feel terrible that I cannot be with her right now".

"Yes. But I'm sure she understands".

"She said she did".

"How is it out at the camp"?

"It is good. There can be one or two chaps who can be annoying, but most of us get on well. The officers are alright too, but a few of the corporals or sergeants can be a bit annoying. I try to mind myself alright".

"Any word yet on when you might be sent over"? Alice spoke with a slight tremor.

John sensed her anxiety and so tried to sound upbeat. "Actually May first, but by the reports we hear there might not be much for us to do by the time we get there".

At first Alice's face froze, her eyes widened and she was speechless. The shock quickly changed to desperation. "That is only next week. Oh! John. Oh! And Rita, she won't be back in time".

John looked down, slumped down his shoulders, and said, "I so much wanted her to be here today too".

Alice put her arm across the back of his shoulders. "Why did they not say anything today in their speeches"?

"I don't know. Probably, they didn't want to upset anyone and for it not to be in the papers".

They then heard Fox's whistle and knew to hurriedly embrace and say goodbye.

"Do come to the boat to see me off, won't you Mum"? His plea sounded more like when he was a boy.

"I love you John. Yes, yes of course I will be there. I love you".

The train clipped along at a good speed again soon after passing Melling on the return trip to Trentham. John sat quietly gazing out over the townships upon which dusk was beginning to settle. He began wondering about how many of the houses he saw had family away at the war or preparing to go like him. Would they ever see their homes again? Some phrases from the speeches he had heard earlier in the afternoon began to recoil in his mind. The crowd's reactions to references of nation, empire and the good fight had stirred him to wonder more about things beyond each day at the camp. It was only a matter of days now before his battalion's departure. His heart sank again knowing Rita was unlikely to be back in time to farewell him on a journey of uncertainty.

Wellington to Egypt, Monday, May 1, 1916

Alice, like many of the people saying their goodbyes, held a hand upon her hat to prevent it from blowing off. Her coat too flipped about. The southerly wind blustered with unwelcome familiarity, as though a bilious sniveling child distracting the crowd from its common devotions. At this time of quickly disappearing precious moments, Alice would rather have been alone with John. Instead she felt hemmed in by the throng and each inadvertent bump and loud voice unnerved her further. At least rain had held off. Her afternoon visit with John had been filled with anxious anticipation of his departure. The pensive mood of the crowd around them was eventually punctuated by a commanding officer ordering all NCOs to prepare the troops for embarkation. When the crowd had quietened the officer then spoke.

"Good day to you all. I am Major Charles Mackesy. I will be the commanding officer for the safe delivery of these reinforcements to Egypt". The major spoke with an unexpected tone. He seemed reflective. "Like my own father, I will take care of your men and women as though they are my own brothers and sisters".

Some in the crowd again began dabbing tears away from their eyes. Some knew he might have been referring to how his father, Lieutenant-Colonel Mackesy, had stood up to his superior British commanders to prevent unnecessary casualties at Gallipoli. Or how his own brother Harry had been killed back in August. "Captain Clark will now say some blessings for all present". The chaplain was brief, but the fitful wind whipped away some of his benedictions from those hanging on to the passage of every word.

Then the slow orderly progression of the Sixth and Twelfth Reinforcements infantry up the gang-ways, each man wearing a lemon squeezer hat and carrying a Lee-Enfield rifle and kit-bag, painfully extended everyone's foreboding.

The Ulimaroa was now on its second voyage since being converted to a troop transporter. It looked unusual with camouflage paint making it stand out among other ships nearby in the choppy water of Wellington's Port Nicholson. Still those other ships, themselves with tall dark chimneys and iron sides, sat steady like earnest attendants in quiet observance of a ceremonial passage. The usual gaiety among their arrivals and departures remained respectfully muted by an unspoken consensus. The Te Anau, a general public ferry from Lyttleton, had arrived earlier in the day with a full complement of soldiers transferring to the Ulimaroa and some on to Trentham Camp. The Rivernia was preparing departure for Sydney and Hobart, the Pateena for Picton and Nelson, and the Awahou for Foxton. As soon as the cranes had finished the loading of harnessed munitions and other supplies, the gang-ways were removed and the Ulimaroa sounded its horn. Alice shuddered at the sudden loudness of the horn. The sound seemed to reverberate right through her aching core in one direction and then echo in the distant other direction of the Hutt Valley. John, like all the other soldiers on-board, waved with his own hat in hand. The ship gradually pulled away guided by a pilot tug boat over the dingy water. The cries from the crowd left behind became a desperate cacophony and an overwhelming noise for Alice. She tried to call out John's name again but her heaving emotion shredded her voice. The ashen sky, tall harbor buildings and cranes on the dock loomed over Alice, who increasingly felt she was trapped in a long dark tunnel; at which other end John moved further away into the dimming light.

John eventually was lost from sight but Alice stood watching the ship for as long as she could. John too had lost sight of his mother, and as he heaved a deep sigh he tried to think of other things. He fixed his eyes on Somes Island and tried to think of the German nationals, possibly some colonials from Samoa too, and of New Zealand born German descendants who were being held captive on the island. He wondered why he was not instead selected to do guard duty there. He wondered some more about how he, being from Wellington, was assigned to the Second Auckland Battalion; just one of the mysteries of the army making its various quotas. Before the ship turned south between Kau Bay and Eastbourne, John looked over toward Seaview and Petone and up the Hutt Valley and he wondered whether he would ever see Trentham Camp again. It was not long before the Ulimaroa had passed the heads into Cook Strait and toward the Tasman Sea on its way to Albany. There it would take on Australian reinforcements too, and then sail across the Indian Ocean to the Suez Canal.

The five week trip to Suez was as boring as it was long. The repetitive daily routine of scrubbing the whole ship helped keep everyone occupied each morning. The fear of infections spreading rapidly had already been a feature of the war, like the dysentery at Gallipoli. John recalled too that there had been a case of meningitis back at Trentham. Fortunately, it was detected soon after the man had arrived and he was quickly isolated. Nearly all the soldiers on board the ship found little to occupy themselves with for the remainder of each day. The 'Monsoon' on-board newsletter took only a few minutes to read, and there were a limited number of books to share too. Many of the men played card game after card game. Despite little space available some of the men still found a way to kick a soccer ball or toss around a rugby ball.

The long route up the Indian Ocean was marked by excessive humidity, which caused many of the men to sleep on the outside decks with varying prostrations and nakedness. The few nurses on board were women and each had already set clear boundaries and so continued to move about the ship, when they had to, with undeterred purpose. The humidity at night time was particularly difficult for some on board who had to remain at stations below deck, for doors and portholes had to be closed when lights were on. Chatter among the men about being closer to Suez reached a peak whenever they saw other ships heading east to Burma and India or south back to Australia and New Zealand. Any revelry, though, fell silent whenever they saw ships heading east so full that patients, some bandaged at head to foot, were also bedded on the decks.

By the time the Ulimaroa had docked at Suez on June ninth all on board had each dressed in their full khaki uniform and were in formation up on deck or lines below deck ready to disembark. John stood with pouches strung at his waist belt and one from each shoulder. His puttees neatly wrapped his lower leg from his boots up and over his jodhpurs. His lemon-squeezer hat, with khaki and red puggaree, was upon his head. Like everyone, he was eager to be on land again and to stroll around with more freedom. The officers and NCOs recognized this too and so allowed everyone to leave their kit bag and rifles for an hour to wander around before next having to board trucks and then a train. The Ulimaroa would await rendezvous with a transporter coming through the canal with wounded soldiers on their return trip to Australia and New Zealand.

The air was hot but dry. To the west John saw hills with an ochre hue. He would learn later they were the Ataga Hills. He could not see any hills to the east. He was surprised firstly with how many of the buildings in Suez looked as familiar as the British colonial buildings in Christchurch, Dunedin, and Wellington. And for that matter Albany too, where he and his fellow soldiers had disembarked on route to go for a march so as to stretch their legs and have tea with that city's mayor. In contrast there stood the Hamza Mosque, with its four minarets standing like sentries each side front and back of a central domed musalla prayer hall. It would be later on in his stay in Egypt that John first got to hear the daily adhan call to prayer. Some street signs had French or English sounding names but they seemed juxtaposed to some of the street architecture. Some buildings had ablaq and acanthus masonry designs that impressed John. He was also intrigued by inscriptions on some buildings that he could not decipher, but appeared to be more than a name or shop signage. As John walked further he saw arcades and gardens bounded by arches and columns. The way many people were dressed seemed unusual to him too. Most men wore a cotton outer garment, with long sleeves, that went from their ankles to a short raised collar. They also wore a head covering held by a cord wound around their head. He would later learn about and wear for himself a thawb and ghutrah. Like many other soldiers, John too would learn to use a combination of a ghutrah and his hat or shrapnel helmet to shade his neck and face from the searing sun. John figured that those people he saw completely covered, and their face too, must be women because he saw none otherwise. He would later learn from one of the nurses that muslim women were required to wear a full burqua when in public. He saw only some people had embroidery on their garments and wondered whether they had some kind of different status. He felt, for the first time in his life, at being at a crossroads of ancient and modern times. Yet the city was quieter than he had imagined. He figured the many guard posts and frequent patrols by British or Dominion troops kept a constant curfew.

The train ride to Ismailia, once beyond Suez and closer to Fayed, gave John and others a bigger perspective of the desert expanse. When the rail line cut back closer to the canal and then the Great Bitter Lake, many of the men remarked on the number of ships waiting. They also noted small fishing boats meandering between the ships and both sides of the lake. One of the officers, who had been to Egypt before, explained to John and others how the canal had no need for locks because it all was at the same sea level. As they approached Ismailia John could see signs of more military presence. Tents and huts were arranged as large encampments. Machine gun posts were scattered along either side of the rail line and at some crossroads. The Union Jack was flying at the railway station and on other government looking buildings. When John and the others had alighted the train, they collected their kit bags and rifles and were then marched down to one of the encampments they saw on the way in. A few veterans of earlier campaigns in Egypt and at Gallipoli were there to greet them, or to get their measure.

"How was the cruise"? asked one corporal with a cheeky tone. Another veteran showed some gratitude, "Great to see you fellows have come to back us up". What was noticeable to John was how some of the veterans who said nothing looked passively through him. They had no glimmer of expression in their faces. He did not have time to think much more about it. His company corporal had shown him and others their tents and the rudimentary ablutions and instructed them to set up space around their assigned bed. After dinner they had to report for parade and roll call.

The morning bugle call came like a bolt of thunder to John's senses. He usually would be at least awakening before the reveille. However, it would take him a few more nights into mornings to overcome the fatigue of travel and adjustment to a different day to night cycle. He recognized that it was Sergeant Francis Lound sounding the bugle. He thought it strange to be reminded about home by hearing the call by the man from Marton out in the Egyptian desert.

Each day John and his unit marched from the camp down toward the canal. They went to relieve other troops from their overnight duty guarding the construction of a new bridge. The first few days on guard duty and watching the construction was interesting for John. He learned it would be the world's largest swing bridge. It only took a week, though, for the guard duty, in trenches surrounded by sandbag revetments and barbed wire, to become tedious. At least his fellow guards had some interesting things to say.

"It was here at Ismailia back in February last year where we had our first taste of battle in this war" said one of the veteran corporals, who had been assigned to guide John and the other new reinforcements. "This is where the brunt of the attack started. Von Kressenstein, a German colonel, led the Ottoman forces. They couldn't come down from the coast or shore of the canal because British and French cruisers would have bombarded them. So they had to cross the Sinai from Palestine; took them ten days, so we had good warning. They carried pontoons too so to be able to cross the canal. But we had dug in well with the Fifth Gurkhas over on the eastern bank. So they had a hard time making a crossing. We lost some chaps, but they lost a lot more. Their retreat was just as bad, having to cross back through the desert".

"Did you know any of our guys who were lost"? John was paying close attention.

"Yes. Willie Ham. He was probably our first loss in this war. He was from around Nelson. He was just twenty two".

John tried to think about the few times he had been to Nelson, but his mind took him back to imagining the battle. Standing next to a canal, in a place with few trees and hotter than he could usually withstand, still seemed somewhat strange to John. It was peaceful though, so he could not imagine the sounds and struggles of the battle. It was easier to instead to look at the light glimmering upon the water in the canal and to remember how the harbor at Wellington would look on a sunny calm day. However, a pit of a feeling had slowly begun to gnaw inside him. He was having a difficult time tolerating the boredom of guard duty, but he did not want to think of what might be ahead of him. Thinking back on days spent with Rita only momentarily satisfied the pit.

The next week though John felt excited about the news that the remainder of the training base and hospitals for the Australian and New Zealand troops were moving from Egypt to England. Relief from the guard duty in the desert could not come fast enough. So he had no hesitation gathering his kit and joining the march to board the train for Alexandria and then a ship for England.

Sling Camp, Bulford, England, Sunday, August 13, 1916

"Dear Rita

I miss you a lot. I hope you got my letters I sent from Egypt about a month ago. We have not gotten any mail from home yet. We are told our mail has probably been held up in France.

I think about what you might be doing there in Wellington, and on Sundays at your church. Have you seen Mr. Crump at all? Do tell him I'd rather be back working for him than be stuck here day after day training on the same things over and over again.

We are now in England. We moved base here about a week ago. We came by ship, the Ivernia, from Alexandria to Southhampton. What a ship too. It has the biggest smoke stack of any I have seen so far. And we saw many large naval ships at Southhampton. It took us eleven days to get here. Going through the Mediterranean and over the English Channel was tough going, not knowing if any German cruisers might turn up. We had English cruisers escorting us though. Then more trains, this time to Amesbury and Bulford. We were crowded into third class. At least they were more comfortable than the Trentham and Egyptian trains. Once off the train we had to march about two miles from Bulford into Sling Camp.

This camp is huge. It houses about four thousand all told. It is called Sling after an old plantation around here. Some of our guys and some Canadians had started building the huts a year ago. It's like being in Trentham or

Featherston. Sure beats being in tents. They are comfortable and each has a Canadian wood stove, which is good because some days are a bit cold and rainy here. My hut is on Malborough Road. Other streets are named after areas back home too, like Nelson, Wellington and Auckland. One is called Kiwi Road too. We have started calling ourselves Kiwis too.

My first days here have not been that good. It is very different from Trentham and the camps in Egypt where we had more Kiwi officers and NCOs than British. Here we have got more Tommie NCOs who bark and snap at everything, everybody. It seems like they are trying to impress upon us that we are somehow inferior. It's a clear case of efficiency run amok. Every day as soon as we crawl from under our blankets we are made to run with a vengeance to the ablutions for a shave and wash. Then we have to run back to the hut to roll up our mattress, just so. Fold our blankets just so. Then sweep the floor, dust the shelves, clean the windows and polish the stove. With those tasks done we then tear around to the mess hut and line up for breakfast with tin mug and plate, knife, fork and spoon in hand and have to march in as a whistle is blown. All the while we have to make a din beating our forks on our plates. With breakfast over we run back to our hut to polish our boots, buttons and rifle and put our full uniform on and be on the parade ground by the next bugle call. It all seems a waste of time.

When we get to do the drills with hand grenades, bayonet charge and rifle practice, that all makes sense. Watching some of the Lewis machine gun crews is impressive. About three miles from here is an aviation school. Every morning and evening there are 6 aeroplanes that fly around. They look great. They are noisy though. I wish I could get a ride in one someday.

It is nice though to see greenery again. The surrounding area is called Salisbury Plains, which is actually more like some of the rolling hills back home in the Waikato or Rangitikei. Today being Sunday we got the day off after 9 am and we can go about five miles without a pass. A group of us went to see Stonehenge. It's just like you see in calendars and postcards. It is amazing to think how the massive stones were put up. You will be pleased to hear we also went to church; actually to just look around at St. Leonard's and then another called The Garrison Church of St. George. Some of the cemeteries here have some very old headstones that go back as far as Norman times. The small villages are nice, all set into the countryside, and you come upon them down hedge row lanes.

No word yet when we go over to the front. They don't really tell us anything until the last moment. I will try and write again before we go.

Love and miss you.

John

The Somme, France, Saturday, September 30, 1916

The month of training at Etaples was even worse than John thought possible after his three weeks at Sling. What must have once been a picturesque enclave, the fishing village and its Northern French coastal surrounds, had been transformed into a massive military complex. The sand dunes and river estuary appeared to John to have conceivably once been the subject of artists. He thought of how before the war the area might have looked much like Waikane, Hokio, and other beaches near Wellington. But he quickly came to curse the dunes for the physical pain and exhaustion wrought upon him from hours of non-stop running up and down on exercises with bayonets and gas masks. The incessant barking of orders by the redcaps, British NCOs with wide red puggarees around their field caps, left John and many other Anzac trainees in startled shock for hours on end. The redcaps' yelling was so close at times that it felt to John their snarling teeth might bite his ear off. He sometimes could feel their spittle spray his face and it took every ounce of him not to retaliate. It stung him to be called a canary at every order, and it certainly felt like being caught in a birdcage that was constantly rattled, surrounded by distorted faces, and blasted with grotesque noise.

John had heard some veterans, among them wounded not fully recovered, wishing to instead return to the front and get out of redcap hell. So the order to pack and march for over-night billeting and then trains to the front at Flers came with strange relief for John. His own pit was growling with dark thunderous feeling but that seemed tame compared to the dogs of Etaples.

It was as though an obscure hand pressed John along on the march and on to the train. The two hundred minute ride, mostly in the dark, was nothing like the many that had conveyed him before. The quintessence of countryside and villages occasionally shone through breaks in the early morning fog outside. So too the mounting signs of lacerated land, broken buildings and harried hospitals strobed through the windows, a portent foretelling. Inside nothing registered on morose faces while only a few other faces flickered with ill-placed silliness. The once distant sounds and tremors of artillery fire could no longer be passed off as the wheels chattering with the tracks. Legs began to shudder, heels to tap, and torsos rock. Heads down or transfixed no one yet looked at the eyes of a fellow passenger. The train slowed, shunted and rattled. A lone quavering voice enjoined few then many as a chorus in singing, Auld Lang Syne. The train halted, and once detrained and in formation one of John's unit called out "Make it a good one boys". The veteran NCOs, this time ignoring the breach, knew too well the anticipation and so joined the impromptu chants breaking out among the men. Then orders were quickly snapped again.

"Alright you chaps, Listen up"! An NCO with a Lancashire accent was yelling out. "You lot here, Second Auckland, I will take you over to join your Battalion over at Gird Trench to the left. Other units, Second Canterbury, Second Otago and Second Wellington, will join their battalions in Grove Alley and other trenches. For you newer guys, if in the thick of things you need to find your Auckland Battalion, remember they too have the same red diamond and black badge as you", as he pointed to John's tunic.

A light rain drizzled through the dense fog and so morning light still struggled to be fully realized. As John marched closer and closer to the front lines he remembered descriptions he had heard from veterans back at Etaples. He began to better understand how hard it was to march in the mud, let alone run when told to hop it because heavy enemy artillery fire had resumed. Not being able to see anything much added to John's neophyte terror at hearing the distant discharges, the whistling projectiles now actually heading toward him, and the uncertainty of where they would explode. Once at Gird Trench he immediately jumped in and crouched low to the ground. His heart was pounding and he gasped for air. He knew that was odd because he was one of the fittest in his unit. He tried to repel putrid smells from his nostrils but that futility gave way to the more urgent need to open his eyes to the reality he was finally at the front.

Looking down at him was a fellow soldier beckoning John to stand up. At first John could not discern from the dirt that covered the man's face and uniform whether he was a friend or foe. The man smiled broadly, cracking more of the drying dirt on his face, and extended his hand to pull John to his feet. "What's your name Kiwi"?

"John".

"Well John, I'm Mike". He continued. "Come stand here, nothing like getting straight into it. Where you from"?

"Actually Wellington, but got assigned to Second Auckland back at Trentham".

"Oh, that's the army for you". And no sooner had he said it a nearby explosion caused him to claps his hands over his helmet to keep it securely on, but he otherwise did not budge.

John had crouched down again, but Mike enticed him back up. "Here, stand here. You will get a great view of the pitch. Except here there's no batting order and the ball explodes on striking the wicket"!

John caught Mike's dry wit and still cautiously stood on an ammunition box and peered over the top of the trench. At first he could not see much beyond the fog. At a short distance he saw five fellow soldiers scurry back from the edge of no-man's land and back into the trench.

"They've been out cutting the wire ready for later. But the fog is starting to lift, so couldn't take the chance of staying out there", said Mike. "Hey, look there"!, as he pointed to show John the fog had lifted very quickly. "There are some huns still out there, some officers too"! "What the....oh, they got it".

John was stunned to see two German officers and around twenty soldiers run but collapse as bullets raked through them. He heard a machine gun, he assumed was a Lewis, over at another distant trench. He had to look away at first. In all the months of training he never actually saw anyone get shot. His thoughts rapidly went through how it happened so quickly. They did not stand a chance. How foolish to be out there like that. Who or what made them do it? When he looked back over he could see one and then another of the fallen Germans attempting to crawl, but awkwardly. The Lewis gun spat out more rounds and both soldiers shook with the impact and then splayed out on the ground.

"Want a smoke"? Mike casually offered a cigarette to John as though nothing unusual had happened.

"Ah, thanks. No, I don't smoke". John stumbled out the words while still shaking off what he just saw. "Where, ah... are you from Mike"?

"Okura Bush. My folks are share-milkers. I worked on the farm and also drove for our local auctioneer".

"Hey! Me too! Well, I drive a milk delivery round in Wellington".

Their conversation was cut short by a corporal rushing through and quietly calling out, "From Lieutenant McClurg, we go in five".

Mike filled in some of the details for John. "We are attacking down on Goose Alley, where the Huns still hold up. We won't be going over the top for a while. Just follow me and you will be right".

John felt pounding in his chest again. His mind swirled with thinking "this is it, this is it. This is it". He at first fumbled at handling his rifle but then repeatedly checked that he had a firm grip around it. His attempts to picture Rita and his mum were foiled by another barrage of incoming artillery explosions and a showering of dirt. The minutes had raced by and Mike signaled for John to follow.

At first John did not understand why they and others ahead of them were just moving along the trench. They had to duck at places where recent explosions had destroyed some of the revetments. They had to jump over legs of guys still being tended to by medical corps and over bodies waiting for stretcher bearers. John's mind continued to race, "this is it, this is it. This is it". And then they paused. "Why"? He thought. He turned and saw many fellow soldiers behind too. Those close by made eye contact with him but all otherwise remained expressionless and quiet. He thought he recognized that some wore insignia of a Canterbury battalion. More explosions shook the ground. The dirt settled again. John was far enough up front to see two guys being helped to strap an unusual large canister on each of their backs. A hose from each canister extended to what looked like a hand held piece of pipe. He had never seen anything like it before and was briefly startled to see each hand held pipe then ignited into producing a short flame. It was like they were welders of sorts. Kneeling a short distance ahead of them were two riflemen exchanging shots with Germans not much further up from what looked like a recent break through into the Goose Alley trench.

From the west and behind John came an even heavier barrage of friendly fire shelling very close by but over nearer to the Germans. The two Auckland riflemen stood back and two other chaps heaved two grenades each and stepped back. Then the first of the flame holders must have pulled something, thought John, because he saw a huge shot of flame. The man moved forward and the flame continued to billow ahead of him into the trench. A few yards in and the second flame thrower took a turn. No return of rifle fire came back at them. As the flame throwers proceeded so too did John and the infantry followed. Explosions of friendly artillery fire advanced another fifty yards. And near the end of each barrage the flame throwers and infantry proceeded further up Goose Alley. It was not far into the trench that John and the others began to see charred bodies of German soldiers. The pungent smell of burnt flesh and hair made John recoil even more than from just looking at the frightful sight. "Poor buggers", he thought. Other Germans attempted to flee up the trench but some were shot as they did so. Some others in desperation to avoid the flames had jumped out of the trench only to be cut down by machine guns.

"That was a real doozy", said Mike to John. "So what did you think for your first jump into the game"?

"It was not what I had expected. Have you seen those flame throwers before"?

"No, that's a first for me too, first time not having to go over the top either. Did you get any shots off"?

"No, no I didn't", replied John with reticence.

"Hey, don't you worry there old chap. You will get your chance sooner than you think.

We are supposed to stay here for now and hold this ground for a day or two. I heard that then we get relieved by another rifle brigade and we head to Fricourt, north east of here. We will exit through Turk Lane, of which the Maori Pioneers have nearly dug through".

The continual exchange of artillery and random sniper fire prevented John and as usual many others from catching much sleep over the next two nights. Rain poured down at various times, day and night. Mud was again knee deep in the trenches. John was also still gripped with anxiety about when his time would come to attack or defend, to get his first shot off. "Will I be fast enough. Will I be accurate enough under the pressure"?, he thought a lot to himself. There were few distractions to relieve the boredom filled by anxiety and hunger waiting for dry rations. But each early morning John could see a single enemy Fokker aeroplane, with large military crosses on its fuselage and wings, doing reconnaissance. He was still intrigued by seeing aeroplanes since his first sighting of the British Sopwith Pups when at Sling. After the enemy aeroplane disappeared German artillery soon opened fire on trenches recently gained by the British. On the second morning, as he and his Battalion were making their way out through Turk Lane, John saw another Fokker being flipped about by the shifting wind. The wind had slowed its flight a bit and so more than one Lewis gun crew spat bullets into the sky that brought down the irresistible target. That spectacle soon lost salience for a while as John and the others with him savored the stew and hot tea that was waiting for them at Mametz Wood. With stomachs better satisfied and rested they then marched to encamp at King George's Hill at Fricourt.

It felt to John that many weeks, not just one, had passed since he arrived at the Somme. Second Auckland had rested for four days but still had to withstand enemy artillery raining down on them. During the late afternoon of October Seventh all the men of the battalion had gathered to hear Lieutenant McClurg address them. "Good afternoon to you chaps. Your rest here at King George's Hill is well deserved. I have here a message of tribute from General Rawlinson, Commander of the Fourth Army".

"I desire to express to all ranks of the New Zealand Division my hearty congratulations on the excellent work done during the battle of the Somme. On three successive occasions they attacked the hostile positions with the greatest gallantry and vigor, capturing in each attack every objective that had been allotted to them. More than this, they gained possession of, and held, several strong points in advance of and beyond the furthest objectives that had been allotted to them. The endurance and fine fighting spirit of the Division have been beyond praise, and their successes in Flers neighbourhood will rank high amongst the best achievements of the British Army. The control and direction of the Division during the operations have been conducted with skill and precision, whilst the artillery support in establishing the barrage counter-attacks has been in every way most effective. It is a matter of regret to me that this fine Division is leaving the Fourth Army, and I trust that on some future occasion it may again be my good fortune to find them under my command".

Not long after the address by McClurg, the battalion dispersed and filed through the mess tents for their evening meal. They then each settled into their own tents for another night of trying to catch sleep between sporadic artillery barrages.

Despite guys in other tents talking after curfew John did manage to drift off to sleep. When the noise of artillery explosions again broke the silence of the night he at first thought he might be dreaming. The fatigue of the past week had caught up with him. He was slow to move. The familiar droning of a shell heading in suddenly got louder and so John dove to the floor and clasped his hands over his head. The blast tore through his tent and along with the shattering ground heaved him into the air. He felt his ear drums and face almost implode. He only briefly recognized he was flying through the air with bits of tent canvas and rope entwined around him. His fearful thoughts, about never seeing his mother and Rita again, barely lasted a half second. John then lost consciousness and so did not feel his body thrashed back down to the ground.

New Zealand Field Hospital, France, Wednesday, October 18, 1916

"Good morning John", said the doctor accompanied by two nurses at John's bedside.

"Good morning sir", replied John.

"Things are looking good John. Your arm is healing nicely. But tell me, how is your head feeling"?

"It's pretty good. The headaches have gone".

"What about your vision and hearing"?

"Both fine, been good for a few days now too".

"How about upon when you stand up, or are just walking around? Do you still feel faint or unstable on your feet"?

"No, that feels fine too". John knew he had to be honest despite it meant leaving the safety of the hospital.

"Alright John, I feel you are ready for discharge. Let's say tomorrow you can rejoin your unit. Good luck to you".

"Thank you, sir".

John had known for close to a week that he was recovering quickly and would be discharged from the field hospital back to the front lines. His thoughts about not having yet fired a shot to attack or defend reverberated almost daily again. The field hospital continued to be besieged with incoming wounded. Death was frequent and so it seemed routine to see stretcher bearers leaving with corpses covered by canvas. John wondered how long it would be before he was more seriously wounded or worse. His thoughts then meandered into what life would be like for Rita and his mother without him around. He hoped they would not mourn for long and get on with daily life. To stop himself from spiraling any deeper into catastrophic thoughts he pulled out of his pack a letter from Rita to read again.

"My Dear John, I miss you so very much. I am constantly praying you will be brought back safe and sound. I cannot wait to wrap you in my arms, to look into your eyes and hear your voice again.

I try not to read the papers or listen to the gossip of what is happening over there. It is hard to know what is reliable and they are not allowed to put details about your company's movements and things like that in the papers. But we did hear about the success of our soldiers at Flers. I wonder whether you were there.

I received your letters from Egypt. It sounded like an interesting place to see, but too hot for me. I am so proud of you for all the places you are seeing and for what you and all our good men and women are doing over there.

We here at home are all trying to do our part too. Your mother and I work at making up ration packs and bundles of blankets and other things. We are also making food parcels through the church auxiliary. We are now making what we call Anzac biscuits. There are some on their way to you now. I hope you get them soon. I think you will like them.

Your mother and Bill have separated again. I think that this will be for good this time. Try not to worry too much about it. I am keeping an eye on her. She is doing well this time. She is keeping busy, especially at the church.

I think she said she has written to you about this too. She has not heard from Emily for a while now. We think she is still in Christchurch.

My mother is doing as well as can be expected. John and Anthony are getting good marks at school and keeping busy with sports. We all still miss my dad so much. I wish I could go down to visit them more often; but having your mother around helps to keep me busy.

Your mother and I went to a play last weekend at the Britannia Theatre. It is the new theatre down on Manners Street opposite Perrett's Corner. We saw "The Divinity of Motherhood". It was about a woman who lived the high life to only find out later as a spinster she had missed out on the joy of having children. It was well done but probably would have been boring for you. We will go to something more of your interest when you are back home. It will be fun. It won't be too long now before I see you again.

Do take care of yourself my love. I think of you every minute of every day.

Rita".

John felt calmer after reading Rita's letter again. He day dreamed about walking with her in Wellington down at the waterfront or up in the Botanical Gardens. He wondered what play or movie they might go to at the Britannia. He did not worry much about the news of his mother separating from Bill Welch. She had gotten on with life on her own before, but John felt also thankful for Rita being there to look after her.

Neuve Eglise, Belguim, Sunday, May 6, 1917

There was a light pounding of one person running, the halting of one foot before the other with a brief silence, followed then by the sound of sticks being struck and one man yelling "How's that"! Then there was a mixture of cheers and jeers. A pause in the exchange of heavy bombardments, warmer weather and a relatively unspoiled field, had encouraged the guys of Second Auckland to attempt a game of cricket.

John sat waiting for his turn to bat and looked around thinking about the guys no longer among them and who would have enjoyed the game. He thought about Mike and his wit and reference to cricket when he first met him in Gird Trench. He missed Mike and came to eventually realize his manner had been not so much about invincibility than inevitability. John himself felt fortunate to have survived various skirmishes with the enemy. One in particular, shortly after he returned to his unit in October, he would not recount to anyone else for a long time. He had sat in his fox-hole, his gun in hand, always waiting for the next bombardment or order to attack or retreat. Another enemy bombardment had begun to rain down upon him and his unit and the order came to pull back. Climbing out of his fox hole, turning his back and running for cover were some of the most frightening moments for John. Fog, smoke or exploded dirt made it difficult to gauge whether any enemy infantry was approaching and might shoot him in the back. The incoming bombardment had progressed another fifty yards and appeared to cut him off from following the same retreat as the rest of his unit. John had to make a quick decision and so dashed to a thicket of trees not yet decimated by explosions. Although more dirt and smoke stung his eyes he managed to sweep back branches he could feel scraping at his head. He thought he had gotten beyond enough tree cover and knelt on one knee to take a breather and tried to figure out a direction in which to go next. He was ready to move again to go find his unit but heard some branches move. He spun around expecting to see one of his unit but instead saw a soldier in gray, not khaki uniform, and with badges of the Kaiser not King George. The German was stunned, as was John. They each grappled for their rifle and the German misfired as he raised his gun and struggled to move the bolt to reload. John had a clear shot but did not pull his trigger. He could see the fear in the other man's eyes. He looked young, thought John. He wondered whether this man too had barely fired any shots before. Neither of them tried to use their bayonets. For a moment they stood frozen not knowing what to do next. John lowered his rifle and without speaking they both seemed to understand that each could retreat without concern that the other would shoot. More bombardments and exploding dirt shattered the area again and within seconds both John and the German went in different directions.

John heard the other guys around him exclaim disappointment as another of their batsmen was caught out behind the stumps. Being deep in thought John had lost track of being the next to bat. Guys on both teams did not hesitate to call out his name and funny remarks to get his attention. Once he realized, he accepted the bat from the returning player and went out to left wicket, the one facing the bowler on the over.

Again the bowler did a long run up and launched an over shoulder delivery and the ball chipped the ground in front of John whose first swing missed. Fortunately the ball travelled too low for the wicket keeper to glove. The bowler then launched another ball that bounced nicely allowing John to stroke it enough to send it out to left field, again too low to catch. He ran to the other end of the wicket and his team mate also at bat made it just in time to the other end avoiding another out. John, however, was surprised by feelings of tightness in his chest and began wheezing. It was such a short run and would not usually bother him, he thought. John's team mate struck bat to ball so well as to hit it beyond the furthest fielder and gave sufficient time for both batsmen to run back and forth again. His wheezing intensified and had him wondering whether he might need to retire from the game. Just as he was about to ask for a replacement batsman an NCO on the sideline called out that an order to stop the game had come down from the commander. The spectators and players alike had ignored the sporadic bursts of shrapnel overhead and the possibility of mortar fire, but the commander could not.

The winter in trenches on the Lys had been harshly cold with persistent rain, and sometimes sleet and snow. John had thought he had come out it feeling very tired but not sick. However, in early April he began to feel soreness in his throat and a cough that he could not suppress by end of the month. His fellow soldiers would sometimes give him scoured glances. They were annoyed by his persistent coughing at night when in their shared tents, or when he was on sentry duty, or they were marching close to enemy lines and silence was required.

John decided to try and ignore the tightness in his chest and so kept reporting for duty each day. Second Auckland, like other battalions in the New Zealand Division, undertook extensive daily practice throughout May near St. Omer, France, in a full-size model in preparation for an attack on the town of Messines, Belgium. At the end of each day Second Auckland, all tired and dusty, marched back to their billets at Esquerdes and leaped into the river there to cool off and wash. It reminded John of his swims in the Hutt River while at Trentham. By the last week of May John and the others knew the time for the assault was very close. He thought it must have also been obvious to the Germans because the traffic of rail carrying infantry and the build-up of tanks and aeroplanes, brought the inevitable noise of military movement. He and the others knew it would be only another day or two before they would again march to the Front. Second Auckland again practiced their attack on the Messines town-ship. They all felt the ominous threat of at last having to practice with respirator masks. John's wheezing intensified and with more running his chest felt like a heavy vice was choking his breathing. He collapsed to his knees, ripped off his mask to reveal his face had turned as though a cerulean cloud.

New Zealand General Hospital, Brockenhurst, England, Tuesday, July 10, 1917

The early morning light had begun filtering through the skylights. It shone as beams upon some beds but not others of the multi-bed ward. It would be another fifteen minutes before the light fully reached the vertically hung Union Jack at the end of the long room. John had awoken and winced again at immediately feeling the pain in his chest, especially on inhaling. He expected that once other patients began stirring and standing there would be the usual morning cacophony of coughing and wheezing. There would be the usual hunching and shuffling in synchrony with more convulsive coughing as patients made their way back and forth to the bathroom.

Once up, dressed and moving about for a while, John felt his lungs working with more ease. The air had warmed up considerably by afternoon so he took his cup of tea to sit outside in the garden. A lone starling was scratching around underneath a nearby hedge while some sparrows flitted about in a small oak tree. They seemed inattentive but were watching and waiting to see whether John might leave crumbs to feed upon. Having hundreds of unexpected flightless visitors brought much opportunity for local birds to feast from unintentional offerings.

John worried that while he was improving his friend Sydney had fallen more ill over the preceding days. He looked down the long lawn hoping to fix his sight and mind on something else. He had begun thinking instead about his mother when he heard a familiar voice behind him.

"Enjoying the fresh air John"?

"Oh. Hello Nurse Blackie. Yes, a nice day isn't it", replied John as the nurse sat down in the chair beside him. Her long grey dress and red cape contrasted against the white wicker furniture. Her gentle looking face was nicely framed by her white veil and high starched collar. She wore her nursing badge upon her white apron.

"How have you been feeling? And, John, you do remember that you can call me Catherine"?

"I am much better thanks. Captain Bowerbank has given me clearance to return home on Saturday. It feels a bit strange to be going with no end in sight here".

"You have given a lot John. You can be proud of what you have done. It's not like you have a choice about going home now. Dr. Bowerbank has decided that for you. It will still take some time before your lungs can function normally again".

John appreciated that Catherine was trying to ease his worry and he knew it all made good sense. It was still hard for him, though, not to think about many of his friends who were not going home - ever. Although he was now many miles from the chaos on the Front or the dogs of Etaples his night time sleep still came in only brief fitful chunks. On most days he shuffled between losing track of time and things once seen replaying in his mind. If not for Catherine reiterating a second time a little more loudly he would have slipped back into staring down the lawn.

"Your Rita and mother will be so very excited to see you. That will be a great moment to finally see each other again".

"Yes, yes it will. I can hardly wait to see them".

"I am also going home in a short while. I am excited to see my family again. My mother has taken ill, so I need to be with her".

"I am sorry. I hope she will be much better by the time you get there. Catherine, some of the guys here have said you are also going home because you, ...your family,... have already lost two brothers"?, asked John with more clarity in his voice and better attention now he could listen to someone else's story instead of being lost in his own thoughts.

"Yes. We are not supposed to say much about our own things", Catherine's voice trembled a little but she had sensed John was now recovered enough to listen. "My own John, he is still okay. He is with the Veterinary Corps. But James and Donald, both younger than John and me, we lost them both at the Somme on the same day last July. It will be one year this Saturday".

"Oh, Catherine, I am sorry. I did not arrive at the Somme until September and heard we had lost a lot of our chaps by then already".

"Thank you John".

"You know, I sometimes wonder why so many other guys were lost but not me".

"There is no rhyme or reason sometimes John. Like I said, you have done your bit and you are now being sent home".

John did not answer and looked into space again until Catherine continued.

"I also wonder why I have been lucky and not others. You did hear about the sinking of the Marquette in October two years ago"?

"Yes! Were you on that ship"?

"So was Dr. Ackland. He drifted in the water for seven hours"!

"Really, I had no idea"?

"Yes. I miss Lorna and Isabel. I miss them all very much. I still do not understand why we had not instead come across earlier on the Grantilly Castle. The Germans do not torpedo hospital ships". Catherine's voice then reduced to a mumble. "I had better get back to the ward".

"Sure. I hope we can meet up back home one day. My mother and Rita would enjoy meeting you".

"That would be nice. Try and stop in to say goodbye before you go".

"I will".

John's pit rumbled again, as the week drew closer to his departure. He looked forward to holding Rita again, and to seeing his mother's effervescent smile again too. But he felt torn. He did not like leaving things unfinished, nor going to the serenity of home while his comrades would be left behind in the chaotic shadow of dismemberment or death. The bells of St. Nicholas had pealed a few hours earlier and had reminded him to go back to say farewell to Sydney. He had been in a bit of a fog when at the churchyard cemetery a few days earlier.

He had not registered much about what then surrounded him. On his second visit he noticed the churchyard felt ancient, let alone the church, with a tower of bricks that seemed to be juxtaposed against older parts Saxon stone and other parts Norman. Old headstones showed the tests of time and weather, with some leaning, some crumbling, and some indecipherable. An old large wide yew stood as sentry over all the cemetery and especially its new charges of around thirty plots. John could see that most of the new white wooden crosses were marked with insignia of the New Zealand Expeditionary Force. Just a few were for Indian soldiers who had been among the earlier wounded visitors to Brockenhurst. Back again at the third row and fourth plot in John could see the soil had been recently replaced. Flickering through John's mind was a photo he had seen of Sydney standing alone with his parents outside their Waihi home. He looked so fresh faced and happy then, thought John. Not the man now interned so far from home his family could never likely visit to pay their respects. Not the man who had waxed and waned between unconsciousness and pain in his lasts days. Not the man whose face and hands had been scarred by cowpox and then acid. Not the man who had withstood the brunt of weapons only to succumb to disease that forebodingly floated stealthily from trench to train to trench.

"Goodbye my friend. You are in a better place now. Say hello to Mike too".

Kaori, Wellington, New Zealand, Thursday, November 28, 1918

What a bittersweet month November turned out to be, thought John. For that matter, it had been a poignant year. He felt warm inside as Rita held his left arm and his skin simmered as they stood together in the bright sunlight. How he yearned over those many months while at the Front or in hospital to be instead closer to Rita. Sometimes vivid in his often distracted mind was his return in August the previous year. How the hospital ship Marama slowly approached the Wellington wharves. How his heart pounded as he recognized Rita and then his mother beside her. Both had waved with such joy and eagerness, even way before they could have possibly seen John himself. From a distance he could not make out who else was standing with them. Gradually features of the person became clearer and as they did so John's bewilderment had turned to disbelief. He had briefly sunk within himself as a question reverberated around in his mind, "Is that my father"? Before leaving the ship he had decided he was too exhausted and would need to ration time with the man he had not seen much over many years. Fortunately his father had stood back for Rita and Alice to briefly monopolize his welcoming with their unyielding hugs and exhilaration. Then his father carefully shook his hand and grasped his shoulder, "good to see you back in one piece son ".

John was reminded every time he saw returned comrades how grateful he was for having all his own limbs. His lungs still labored but the home air felt good. He was not so sure, though, about his mind. Night after night came with him tossing and turning, while fragments of the war replayed unrelentingly whether he was awake or asleep. Although he tried he often could not avoid hearing news of the war. Seeing headlines was enough to instigate more broken images. Shortly after he had arrived home there were rumours of a mutiny at Etaples. John's pit would rumble like thunder again as he tried to resist memories of the redcap bully-dogs. He easily imagined how much more intolerable it must have become, especially for those so loyal yet from so afar, to be tormented by the pernicious pretenders. He had also heard of the loss of Tui Haswell at the battle of Ayun Kara, Palestine, in the previous November. He had enjoyed watching Tui and the others of the Auckland Mounted Rifles practice at Trentham, and then again in the Egyptian dessert. How he had enjoyed Tui whistling as though he was the actual bird. However the memories of seeing horses falling under fire and the noise of their demise then echoed in John's mind for days. They shut out the good memories of the friends he had made.

Even after Christmas and his birthday on Easter weekend had come and gone, John felt each day he was still juggling the many pieces of himself. He was thankful though to Crump for easing him back into his morning milk round for his newly named City Milk Supply company. Meandering through the familiar streets at a quiet time of day was more helpful than John could put into words. He still preferred to mostly keep to himself, other than be with Rita and his mother. Conversing with his father did not come easy, as much as his father tried. Behind every conversation John wondered why he had reappeared in his mother's life. Were they both grasping the failed familiar to fend off feared loneliness. Yet they had not yielded to living under the same roof again. John thought it was sometimes easier to smile and nod as though listening to his father's attempts to retell some past glories or family days in Christchurch.

John's father at least heeded Rita's advice not to press him about details of the war. That gave only some relief as news of the war was still difficult to avoid, from papers left around the milk depot, at home, or read by other passengers on the trams. In August the New Zealand brigades had taken Grevillers and Bancourt. In September they attacked Crevecoeur and on November fourth they stormed Le Quesnoy. Then on the twelfth such excitement and celebration broke out in Wellington, and all parts of New Zealand, upon hearing about the Armistice. John, however, remained detached. His thoughts were on his comrades still at the Front, of what they were doing and of what they were saying. How at that moment he wanted to be there instead.

John briefly oriented again to Rita standing beside him, holding his arm, and again to the warmth of the sun. Her voice broke through his distraction. "John dear, are you alright"? He nodded while looking around. He saw headstones and plots and momentarily had to remind himself he was not back in the church cemetery at Brockenhurst. He looked down and remembered it was only a few days earlier he had watched his father's casket lowered into the ground there at his feet. There had been no church service, just a quick committal at the grave side of plot number One Hundred and Eighteen E in the second of the Church of England sections. In the prior few weeks he had entertained keeping more company with his father to only then see him too succumb to the unseen enemy that was influenza. His father's isolation at the St. John's Temporary Hospital left no choice for John. Any chance of renaissance in their relationship suffocated along with his father. John wondered whether he himself felt anything or was instead numbed by the practicality used in managing death in the war. Now at home, he had not expected to see the same methodical waltz with death. But every day since October he had heard of so many people being isolated and then dying. The Reaper did not harvest at such pace and stealth even at the war. John's mind drifted from being in the chaos at the Front to seeing ambulances and hearses in the quietness of early morning in Wellington. His mind replayed the tearful words of Rita's friend, Anahera, say her whanau were losing so many there was "no time for tangi".

Rita gently tugged John's arm to signal for him to walk with her. He knew his feet were walking but he could not feel them move across the ground. He felt surreal, as though some force other than himself glided him along. He had no sense of how long they had been walking by the time they came to the public section of the cemetery. There were tens of new graves in the second section. There had not been enough time to erect proper headstones, only plot markers. He and Rita stopped at an open plot marked as number Three Thousand, Three Hundred, and Eighty One. A coffin was ready to descend. John recognized the minister and a few members from his mother's Spiritualist Church, who greeted him and Rita. There too was Anahera, but John could only again muster a brief "hello". Upon seeing Rita's signal the minister then began the prayers of committal. John could hear the minister's voice but he could not register most of the words. Even the words "accept into your ever-lasting world our sister Alice" did not seem to outwardly affect John. But he did hear his mother's name. How strange that seemed to him. He had forever barely thought about using her actual first name. She was "mother" as far as he and Emily were concerned. It was not strange that Emily was not among the gathering. John could understand why Emily or anyone might be reluctant to travel while the invisible malady still spread misery. She simply remained in Christchurch. John imagined his mother was back at the Riddiford Street, Wellington, home preparing afternoon tea for these few visitors, like she did many a Sunday. There would be small tomato or cucumber sandwiches, freshly baked scones, and, of recent new recipe, Anzac biscuits. How much better they tasted fresh than they had weeks later in Egypt or Europe.

John sharply shook his head as though to disperse in his mind the image of the Normal School Temporary Hospital. He had driven past that school in Thorndon many times before the epidemic. The sights and sounds of the busy school children replayed through his mind.

The photo of Norah, Rita's much younger sister, flickered in his mind too. He remembered feeling odd and unable to console Rita, but questioned himself was that last week or some months ago. His mother would help him remember what had happened. She had only gone to convalesce at the school and visitors were not permitted. But she was back home by now, he convinced himself. How silly it is that she is not here with her friends, he thought. On the upcoming Sunday she would be preparing to attend her church, just like she had year after year as far back as John could remember. It went without saying that Sunday was her day; a day away from the usual chores of preparing meals ahead of each few days, many a time for borders, washing and hanging out clothes, and cleaning the house and then cleaning at other people's houses. She welded an axe to cut firewood too, until John and Emily were old enough to do it. John still looked blankly ahead as he recalled playing in the kitchen of their Kilmore Street home and seeing his mother shovel coal from a tin bucket into the wood-fire stove. He remembered how Emily often helped him retrieve or return his box of toys from a cupboard. He liked the few small caste iron trucks, animals and soldiers that his mother had received from Mrs. Tonks. He was pleased he had kept them and wondered which box they were still in. He might look for them as soon he and Rita get home. His mother would not mind. She would be busy with her friends and afternoon tea.

Wellington, Tuesday, January 28, 1919

The rain and southerly wind persisted in Wellington, like in many parts of the country. But that did not dampen Rita's excitement. "You look handsome John", she said. She was remarking on how he looked in the suit from Kirkcaldie and Stains, lent to him by Crump. She reached to touch his yellow tie and then realized it did not need adjustment. She instead ran her fingers lightly down his vest, which sat a little loosely under the similarly colored black jacket. Although the pant leg was tapered the waist felt a little too big to John. His belt helped though and nicely matched his polished black leather shoes. He appreciated that Rita's fussing was part of how she liked to take care of him. He knew too she had taken care of the details for this special day and week, like she had for their Christmas. He looked at Rita and was grateful for how it felt to be smiling again. He liked how he could think about a future better than the past few years had been. "You look beautiful Rita", said John. He stood and appreciated how she looked in her cream V-neck blouse with collars that flowed over the V-shaped lapels of the dark brown outer jacket, and a matching ankle length velvet skirt, belted high at the waist. She wore a borrowed brown derby hat, upon which she had attached three small Aglaia roses, and from under which her deep brown eyes sparkled as she also smiled.

Their moment of smiling must have seemed infectious, in a nice kind of way, to the few guests present. They all looked and smiled at John and Rita with their own peaceful awe. Crump was there and admired how his suit looked on John. There too was Anahera and some of the same friends from the Spiritualist Church. The same minister stood ready to preside once more.

"We call upon God's love to bless this special gathering. We have come together to witness John and Rita confirm their commitment and trusting in each other, to know that they will be beside each other regardless of what comes their way; be it good and wonderful things or challenges and uncertainty. It is our responsibility as a circle of community around them to support John and Rita as they make their vow of unity today and be together hereafter. Please take each other's right hand and affirm these vows as I now read them. John, you go first. I commit myself to you Rita, to care for your comfort and needs, in times of happiness and sadness."

As John repeated those words he felt himself breathe easier and gazed into Rita's eyes. The minister continued with more statements for John and then for Rita who repeated the same vows and finished with,

"I love you John as my closest friend and will stand beside you always".

The minister indicated for each of them to hand their rings to him and then said, "These rings are the symbol of unbroken circles, of the unbreakable love between all married people, and of the wider circle of community around us. It is with these rings you each say to the other that you live now unified as one unending circle of love. As John placed one ring on Rita's finger he repeated the vow, "Rita, I give you this ring as a symbol of my eternal commitment to love, cherish and respect you".

Rita took the other ring and as she placed it on John's finger she repeated the same vow and added with a warm smile "with all my heart, darling". To which the guests took a collective sigh and the minister briefly paused to appreciate the moment and then continued.

"I now have the honour to announce that John and Rita henceforth go as husband and wife, and say they can seal their commitment with a kiss. To those present here and to all others in the world I give you Mr. and Mrs. Bowen. Go in peace with love and joy in your hearts".

Crump, Anahera, and the others present stood and applauded. They all then followed John and Rita, still full of smiles, into an adjoining room in which a small afternoon tea reception had been arranged. While John and Rita enjoyed the company, and repeated congratulations from their guests, they were both secretly looking forward to having their time alone.

The overcast weather had not improved any by the time evening arrived, but that mattered not to John and Rita. They had each been anxiously anticipating this night to revere in each other's physical presence, and to slowly consummate their love through efflorescent caress and whispered charms. With the borrowed suit, hat, and other clothes set aside, they momentarily admired each other's physique and then rushed into emphatic embrace. Rita reclined her head backward as John kissed the nave of her neck and his left arm fetched against her back. Their embrace transformed into lithe entwinement and their passion lifted each other to heights neither had felt before. As they lay together, still embracing but at rest, they again exchanged endearments and chatted excitedly about their future. The need for sleep eventually interceded with Rita snuggled close to John.

John and Rita appreciated the sleep and then lying awake late into the next morning. The excitement and organizing of the previous few days had tired them both, but now they were looking forward to taking the ferry to Port Chalmers, Otago that afternoon. It would be a honeymoon of sorts, spending much of the time at Rita's family home but at least some time alone on walks and relaxing at the beach. They both knew there would be some sad remembrances of family now gone, but this was a trip of celebration too with her mother and brothers. A time to cheer together for family now and to come, thoughts they both shared without directly having to say.

The afternoon arrived and the blustery weather continued and promised a rough sailing. John had preferred to not have to take the SS Marama, because of the obvious reminders of it having carried him back from the war. But the very late night sailing of the SS Monowai had deterred Rita, to which John had quickly come around to agreeing with. John's apprehension further disappeared once they had left the wharf and he felt Rita at his side. The views of Somes Island and down the Hutt Valley, only as far as the rain and mist would allow, did not carry the same connotation as they had when he had sailed to the unknowns of the war. He instead pictured himself with Rita at those places. Perhaps they might venture out to the races at Trentham one day after they return, he thought.

Despite persistent rain and wind making the sea quite choppy the Marama still made good time over Cook Strait and down the east side of the South Island. John and Rita well withstood the constant lurching of the boat. For most of the sailing they took comfort in the large public lounge, which had soft sofas and walls made of fine timber. To John, the ship looked as though it bore no signs of having been a hospital transport during the war. He and Rita became more thankful though they had not waited to take the Monowai. A crew member of their ship informed them that heavy rain in Wellington had closed the docks and led to postponing the Monowai's departure until the following day. They were disappointed in their summer so far, but were hopeful about their visit to Rita's family. The Marama eventually drew closer back to the coastline and to the entrance of the Otago habour. So John and Rita buttoned their jackets and went to an outside deck so they could get a better view. John could see what appeared to be a manmade breakwater, and behind it was a small village on one land spit. A larger peninsula opposite to the spit and village formed the other side of the harbor mouth. After the steamer passed through the mouth John could see some marshes that looked so unusually white. Almost like low swept dunes he had seen in coastal parts of Egypt. Rita explained to him that they were salt marshes. As the steamer progressed into the harbor John could see that the ridges on both sides rose higher. Then another smaller hilly peninsula and two nearby islands looked like gates that divided off an upper harbor further in, atop of which John knew Dunedin was located. This reminded John of the narrowing of the Hutt valleys at

Silverstream and Stokes, but these Otago valleys had instead been drowned by the sea. Rita also explained to him how in earlier days Port Chalmers had been a busy immigration entry point into the country. The islands, Quarantine Island and Goat Island, had been used to hold and process immigrants. At other times they held any passengers or crews of ships with suspected infectious diseases.

The steamer slowed its engines and began to turn and glide toward the wharf at the bottom of the hilly peninsula. Berthed on one side of the wharf was another ship of similar size, the SS Maunganui. Unknown to John and Rita it was awaiting another voyage to repatriate New Zealand troops from Europe. They could then see Rita's two younger brothers, John and Anthony, waiting for them as their ship carefully pulled up to the wharf. The two brothers had been anxious to meet John, and immediately Rita could tell they were treating him with some reverence already. Anthony insisted he carry their one large suitcase to the Studebaker car they had borrowed from a neighbor and had waiting for them. John quickly recognized to accept the offer from an eager younger man. He also admired the car with its four front lights and thick leather upholstered seats. He saw on one inside panel there was a small brass badge which noted S.R. Stedman of Dunedin being the local dealer of Studebaker automobiles. It was just a short drive to the family home further around in Carey's Bay. The Victorian house looked as familiar to John as many other city hillside houses in New Zealand, and its outlook was just like others in the various bays of Wellington. The large front entry had rectangular panes of embossed colored glass in the surround and in the top part of the door itself. The door opened and a woman he knew from photos to be Rita's mother, Ellen, rushed out with welcoming arms wide open.

"Oh Rita, you're home! I have missed you so much"!

"Oh Mum!" said Rita as she dabbed her teary eyes.

John was moved by seeing Rita and Ellen's intense embrace and so had quietly waited to greet and be greeted. Ellen took a second to gather herself and then turned to John and placed her hands on his arms.

"John, I am so happy to finally meet you. The boys and I have been looking forward so much to having you in our home".

"I am so happy to be here. It feels so great to finally meet you all". But John wondered some more about how well he might get on with Rita's family now he was actually there.

Ellen had prepared them a hearty dinner of hot corned beef and white sauce over potatoes and leaks. She had expected their travel had made them extra hungry. Rita's brothers had been patient waiting on the delayed dinner, and still showed restraint as their mother suggested John and Rita be the first served.

"We thank God for taking into his care all our loved ones now with him in heaven. And we thank him for this good food that we all still here share". she said.

After dinner, Rita and Anthony assisted their mother with cleaning up and making tea while the two Johns retired to the sitting room. The brother John liked how his brother-in-law was taking interest in family photos and things, and so answered his many questions.

"This was taken four years ago. This is my dad, my mum, and Rita. That is Anthony and me. That is our Norah". He hesitated a little, then, "We lost her last June".

"I am so sorry". John looked a little closer at Norah in the photo and then did not want to bring up too much of the last year and so changed the subject. "What about this one"?

"That is my father's parents and grandparents. It was taken some time ago in Portugal and my dad brought it with him here to New Zealand".

"That is interesting. The frame even looks a bit different from what you usually see from around here. Have you heard about how the civil unrest is going on in Portugal "?

"Yes, it has been in our papers too and in the few letters we have gotten from my Dad's relatives. Sounds like they might reach some sort of peace this week."

"Did your father enter New Zealand right here at Port Chalmers"?

"Yes he did. I presume you saw the two islands out in the harbor"? asked Rita's brother.

"Yes I did".

"My dad, like other immigrants, was held on one of those islands for some time until given official approval of entry. You might be interested to see this too", said the brother pointing to a framed certificate on the wall above an upright piano.

"What is it"?

"It is the certificate of my father's naturalization to become a New Zealand citizen".

John looked closely and read excerpts of the certificate. "Whereas Antonio Cabral of Carey's Bay, Port Chalmers in the Dominion of New Zealand, fisherman, being a person of good repute, hath duly presented to me a memorial praying that letters of naturalization may be granted to him, and a certificate as by law is required, and hath since duly taken the oath prescribed by the Alien Act of nineteen o eight". John paused for a breath and then read another excerpt. "Antonio Cabral shall hereafter have and enjoy all the rights and capacities which a natural-born subject of the United Kingdom can enjoy or transmit within the Dominion of New Zealand; Given under the hand of His Excellency the Right Honorable Arthur William de Briton Savile, Earl of Liverpool, Governor and Commander-in-Chief in and over His Majesty's Dominion of New Zealand and its dependencies, this tenth day of March, in the year of our Lord, one thousand nine hundred and thirteen".

Rita was silently pleased to see her brother and husband were getting along when she, Anthony and Ellen, arrived with trays of cups and food for tea. The remainder of the night before bedtime was passed with chatter about local town gossip and questions to John about goings on in Wellington. Then Ellen announced she had prepared Norah's room for herself and the master bedroom was ready for John and Rita, also suggesting it was time for bed. John immediately declined the master bedroom, thinking Ellen had done it just out of politeness, and so said " Oh, no. We shouldn't put you out like that"! But Rita knew better and tapped John's arm to indicate it was alright. She knew her mother was in her own way acknowledging that they now represented the future of the family, "Thank you mother".

The next day was still overcast and John and Rita were surprised to read in the daily paper that snow might be expected for the highest South Island peaks. However, they decided to still take a walk so Rita could show John around her home town. Her immediate interest was to show John where her father had worked out of as a fisherman. Down at the bay mist lingered like a thin veil over the water, the boats bobbing in the water, and the buildings on the shore. Rita explained where her father's boat had been regularly berthed, how he would have taken some of his daily catch of moki and cod to the Miller's Brothers for curing, and of his calling into the general store beside the Crescent Hotel for flour and other goods to take home.

Rita paused briefly and to John she seemed momentarily sad. She was likely thinking something about her father, he thought. She just as quickly perked up and said, "I was on my father's boat right here when his friend Piripi told me how the Maori, before any Europeans were here, had called this place Koputai. I remember how well he told the story about what it meant, of how some very tired warriors had taken rest on the shore and while asleep a high tide quietly washed their canoes out into the bay. It feels kind of strange to think my father no longer comes down here; and how strange it must feel for John to come down here too. That boat-house over there belongs to John's rowing club".

As John and Rita continued to walk she told John how only fifty or so years earlier, because of the Otago gold rush, the port was one of the busiest in New Zealand and Australia. Then in the 1882 ships with refrigeration first began carrying frozen meat out of Port Chalmers to England. When Rita and John came to the corner of Beach and George Streets Rita pointed out the post office where she had sometimes gone to mail letters for her father. She smiled too at remembering her father's excitement whenever they received a letter from his old home country. John noticed that Rita's enjoyment at being his personal guide had picked up again and so he reacted by placing a kiss on her cheek. With gleaming eyes she reciprocated with a kiss to his lips.

Rita then led John to show him the Saint Joseph's Convent School. There stood an impressive new looking two-story brick building, and Rita explained how it was Anthony and Norah who had mostly attended there. She and her brother John though had mostly attended at the prior old building. That building was an old house that had been converted by Sister Mary Mackillop and her Josephite sisters from Australia twenty one years earlier. Rita was enjoying thinking about her time at the school and so excitedly told John "in one year I received first place in standard five and John won a prize for singing".

Sensing though that John had possibly had enough of seeing places and buildings of the port, Rita then suggested they return home. So John agreed, thinking he was in need of a cup of tea and a bite to eat.

After dinner Ellen asked Rita to play some on the piano. Rita was at first hesitant.

"Go on dear", repeated Anthony with a lilt to goad her.

Rita grabbed Anthony's arm as she had many times with her brothers when they playfully teased each other. Once at the piano Rita deftly laid her fingers to the keys and played with such grace of which John had not heard before. The sound of Brahms' Lullaby drifted from the piano and carried throughout the house. John was impressed and so insisted Rita play some more. She obliged with playing Beethoven's Fur Elise and then Moonlight Sonata. "Alright, I think it is John and Anthony's turn to entertain us", said Rita of her brothers. She sorted among sheets of music to find a booklet of songs. "Ah, found it", and placed it on the music rack. John could see the title read Cancao de Coimbra, and not knowing what it meant he was interested to hear what the brothers would sing. Rita remained at the piano and began a melody John had not heard before. The first brother, John, started signing and gradually showed the strength of his tenor voice through the first verse and chorus. It must be Portuguese, thought John. Anthony then joined in for the second verse with a clear alto voice. John was impressed and then more so when Rita and Ellen also joined in for the second chorus and all four completed the song together.

"Antonio and the girls would have loved this", said Ellen wistfully. "He would have played his guitar".

Rita and her brothers agreed. John though was at first puzzled by Ellen's reference to another girl besides Norah and Rita. He then remembered Rita had once told him her sister Hilda had died as a baby. He was thankful he had not awkwardly asked in the moment. John had ignored his tiredness while enjoying the music but readily agreed when Rita suggested they retire to bed. Her mother and brothers followed suit.

The following morning after breakfast Rita, John and her brothers accompanied Ellen who wanted to visit the family plot at the cemetery not far from their home. Most of the walk was uphill but Ellen seemed to manage it well. Both she and Rita carried flowers to place at the plot, while Anthony took along a rugby ball. He jostled it in his hands with the hope they might at some point later take time to play some footy. When they arrived at the plot John and the brothers stood back a little to firstly allow Ellen and Rita to stand each side of the grave, pray their silent respects, and then place their flowers. After a few minutes the two women quietly moved back a little to allow the two brothers to approach more closely. Rita went and hooked her arm through John's who still stood respectfully back at the bottom of the plot. Nothing was said between them all until Ellen remarked,

"How the girls love their father, and must be so happy to be with him now too".

Rita nodded and added, "How father loved the sea. This is such a perfect spot to remember them by".

Not much else was said between them all, and to John they each seemed to be reflecting in their own way and so he respectfully kept quiet. Ellen then kindly gave them all permission to not worry about her walking back home by herself and to continue their own fun for the day; so the four of them set off to walk further to see the cairn for Robert Falcon Scott. John was impressed with the expansive views from the memorial and to read how Scott had visited Port Chalmers a few times but in November 1910 it was his last before he and his team perished in the Antarctic. John then asked about a ship that was anchored out in the stream of the harbor.

"Why is that ship waiting out there"?

Anthony was eager to display his knowledge and so immediately replied while retrieving the ball he had just tossed up in the air.

"That is the Verdun. It just arrived this morning from Newcastle. It's out there waiting for the port health inspector to give it clearance. It is here to load on wool to take to the United Kingdom".

"This place is busier than I imagined", replied John. He then had some fleeting memories each of Suez, Alexandria and Southampton ports. He shrugged those memories off quickly though as he did not want any more intruding on the good time he was having with Rita and her brothers.

Anthony then suggested again they should go pass the rugby ball around. The others agreed and so they headed down Brailleys Track and Church Street and other streets to the recreation park at the southern part of the town. At one end an old pavilion looked in much need of repairs but the grounds themselves seemed a good pitch thought John. They all took off their shoes and socks and began to jog around tossing the ball back and forth. After a while they tired of just passing and so began punting the ball too. The younger brothers had more stamina and so kept it going for longer than John and Rita, who sat for a breather. While watching his brothers-in-law John started to recognize how quickly he had become comfortable with Rita's family.

"Your brothers are nice guys", he said when they had a brief moment alone.

"It will be hard leaving tomorrow". Rita felt an ache in her stomach and chest.

To which John wrapped his arm over her shoulders and gently pulled himself against her.

Carey's Bay, Port Chalmers, New Zealand, Saturday, January 31, 1920

Water wept off oars that were swiftly lifted, feathered, and then stroked downward in unison to again catch the high tide water of Carey's Bay. The four rowers inhaled and then exhaled a collective whoosh with each propulsion of the boat. The creaking oarlocks were the only inharmonious sounds for the one and half mile practice run back to shore. Warm humid air of late morning clung heavily to the rowers. They might have instead preferred the northeasterly breeze at their backs. Although the breeze was coming down the coast it was being moderated by the surrounding ranges.

After reaching the jetty of the Port Chalmers Rowing Club the rowers climbed from the boat and then again in unison lifted it quickly out of the water. Thompson, their coach, asked them to gather around.

"Congratulations to you all again for being chosen as the Otago representative crew for this coming Wednesday's challenge of Southland for the Edmond Shield. We have not had this challenge since nineteen fifteen, and as you likely know we've had a mighty good record since the first race in nineteen o one. So we will be very pleased to see the shield come back home here to its rightful place".

"Here, here"! cheered the crew.

"Then Friday week, it has been confirmed, the annual regatta will be held this year at Dunedin. We have put on a good show here at the port for many years, but this year the association decided to participate along with the swimming carnival and other events in the city".

"We hear that the Avon club guys are the ones to beat", said Colthorpe, the oldest and more experienced member of the port crew.

"Well, we will see", replied Thompson. "They practice a lot on their river, so it remains to be seen how they will handle the upper harbor".

Each of the crew mumbled some agreement with Thompson who then quipped

"So Anderson and Hoskins, I believe it is your turn today to clean and put away the boat", to which they both reluctantly agreed and walked away to do so.

Thompson then asked Colthorpe and John, Rita's brother, to stay with him.

"John, how are you doing? It looked like you were laboring a bit out there. What do you think James"?

"Yes, I thought so too John", said Colthorpe.

John thought for a moment and then responded. "I thought I was doing fine until we reached Athfields. I just could not push as hard as I usually can".

His face showed frustration so Colthorpe put his arm over John's younger shoulders and said, "John, you are great member of crew. I can see you competing for many years yet to come, but you may need to rest for this one on Wednesday".

"I can see you are disappointed and worried about letting the crew down. I can ask the Queen's Drive guys to lend us someone like Sunderland", said Thompson, whom quickly added, "And, by golly, we will need you all ship shape for the regatta".

John nodded in quiet agreement. He then dropped his shoulders as though acknowledging to his coach, Colthorpe, and himself that he could not even muster the energy to dispute what they were saying.

"Let me give you a ride home John". Although the walk to and from home was something John regularly did, he gratefully accepted Colthorpe's offer.

Ellen noticed John was quiet but he did not complain or say anything about being rested from the crew. He ate dinner and desert and quietly read until retiring to bed. The next morning Ellen wondered why John had not arisen out of bed in time for breakfast and then church. She knocked lightly on his bedroom door.

"John, John. Are you up"? She got no reply so she stepped into the room and stood by his bed.

She called to John a little louder and then moved to touch his shoulder. He gave no response though, to which Ellen felt a sense of dread come over her. She screamed for Anthony who came running.

"What, what is it"? Anthony then also tried to rouse John but got no response. "Mum, he is breathing, but strangely, and he feels very hot"!

Anthony ran to borrow and bring the neighbor's Studebaker car to the front of the house. He then helped his mother carry John under his shoulders down the hallway and out of the front door. Their urgency demanded and found the strength they needed to get him from the house and into the car. Ellen then climbed into the back seat while Anthony hurriedly drove west across town to the port's Cottage Hospital. It was a fine morning and the sun reflected brightly off the white exterior and red roof of the small hospital. It shone like a beacon on the rise above Mussel Bay Station and Anthony drove as fast as he could toward it. Fortunately there was little or no carriage or car traffic between church services. When they arrived at the hospital they at first struggled to get John from the front seat but again urgency gave them strength. The nurse on duty had noticed their arrival and had immediately gone to hold the door open for them to enter. She indicated for them to take John through the small lounge and into one of the two vacant bedrooms. She assisted Ellen and Anthony to lay John down in a comfortable position and she then quickly left to phone the local doctor.

Rita had been home a few hours after returning from attending her church in Wellington. She was busy with pots and lids in preparing an evening meal and so at first did not hear the phone out in the front hallway. On its fourth ring she picked up the receiver and had barely finished saying hello when she heard her mother's tremulous voice announce how her brother had suddenly taken ill.

"Oh my poor John", said Rita with her own trepidation at immediately being reminded of the sudden loss of other family. "Mum, I will come down", she promised without hesitation or thoughts of when and how.

Rita was concerned the next morning when she discovered that no inter-island ferries were scheduled for Port Chalmers at all in the forth-coming week or so, and only one, the Monowai, was scheduled for Dunedin the following weekend. So she quickly arranged to take the SS Maori sailing that night, Monday, February Second, to Lyttleton and then train travel to Dunedin on to Port Chalmers.

It was Tuesday morning by the time Rita arrived at Carey's Bay. Her brother had worsened according to her mother. He had gone into a deeper coma, his breathing more erratic and his face and body had darkened. A sign that influenza, although not as rampant, had not yet finished its gouging of the ingenuous. He must be fighting as hard as he always did at work and sport, they all thought and shared. He hung in for day after day for fifteen more days. When his breathing finally stopped a nurse came out to the hospital lounge to inform Rita, Ellen, and Anthony. Her lovely handsome boy had gone, thought Ellen who collapsed into Rita's arms. Her utter fatigue overwhelmed any apparent distress. Anthony held Rita's right shoulder to help support the load and ease them both down to the sofa; as he did so he could no longer hold back his tears that had been welling for days. Rita closed her eyes briefly in disbelief and then her tears rained down her face too and onto her mother.

Rita phoned her husband, as soon as she and Anthony had assisted their mother to her bed back at home. John could immediately tell the news was the worst when he heard the quivering of Rita's voice. He felt bad for not being there with Rita and her family but told her he would take the seven fifty eight pm sailing that night on the SS Wahine to Lyttleton. He said he would take the same train travel as Rita had and be at Carey's Bay the next morning.

While riding the train John found an Otago Daily Times from the day before. He was at first amused to read how, at the Lambton Quay Tea Rooms in Wellington, a soda fountain had unexpectedly exploded. While it caused damage and drenched the tea rooms no one was injured. John was then taken a back to read how a young man, Lester Cliff, had been drowned at St. Clair Beach, Dunedin, on the prior Saturday. The beach had been crowded but valiant attempts to save the man from the heavy seas failed. John felt sad for the man's father who, according to the paper, got the bad news while away on holiday. On the next page he came across death notices, and at first tried to ignore them. But the urge to look for his brother-in-laws name drew him in to read further. He did not find John's name but he read some more. He was further saddened to see that another young person of Port Chalmers, Violet Emerson, had died at her parent's home, on Scotia Street, just three days before. John decided to put down the paper rather than be further affected by sad news.

By the time he arrived at Carey's Bay John too was exhausted but immediately had to go into support mode for Rita. She leapt to hug him when he walked in behind Anthony, who had met him at the station. She began crying inconsolably and would not let go of John. He cradled her head with his right hand and left shoulder, and stroked her hair as he did so. He looked and saw that the kitchen and dining room were full already of wreaths and bouquets of flowers, and of baskets of food. After a short while Rita had gathered herself and then suggested to John she take him to see her mother, who was dressed but again laying on her made bed. Ellen allowed John to lean across and embrace her while he stated his condolences. As he stood back again Ellen quietly asked him how his travel down had been, to which he replied it was long but had gone well. She next asked about how his job was going. John could tell that the small talk was Ellen's way of trying to engage in conversation again. It was though she knew what would be expected of her the next day at the funeral service and reception. He told her about how his milk deliveries had picked up again now more folk were back from the war. He told her how his boss, Crump, had sent his condolences too. "He sounds like a good man", Ellen said and John agreed. Ellen then dropped her head and Rita touched John's left arm, but he had already recognized that Ellen was indicating she needed to be alone once more.

The following day the priest delivered a resounding sermon on the glorious passage from human frailty to ever-lasting life in heaven. But the somber mood of the gathering remained as palpable as the heavy smell of incense that hung in the air. At the close of the service the coffin was hoisted to the pall bearers' shoulders and carried down the aisle. It was followed by Ellen with Anthony, Rita with John, and then others filing out in respectful order. At the front entryway boys and men wearing colors of the port rugby and rowing clubs, and Queen's Drive Rowing Club, had formed an honour guard all the way down to the awaiting Ford hearse of Love Brothers. It was a slow procession of cars and carriages. Anthony again drove his family in the neighbor's Studebaker, and followed the hearse further up and across the hill to the cemetery to plot one hundred and fifteen. The family plot had in the morning been prepared to receive another of the Cabral fold.

A moderate southwesterly breeze flowed down from the upper harbour and swept over the peninsula as though to dry the northeasterly rain that had anointed the ground the day before. As the priest performed the internment prayers, Ellen thought of her Antonio, Hilda and Norah smiling as they saw and took the hand of their son and brother. Anthony was still intensely missing his brother, and was holding back tears while trying to look strong among the gathering at the graveside. Who would he chide for fun each day and then enjoy rough-housing with or play footy with at a moment's notice. Rita held her John's arm and felt her heart ache for her brother, father and sisters. She worried about Anthony and how he would cope without his older brother now too. How could she take care of him and her mother when she and John return to Wellington.

John at first felt it strange how he had visited this family plot only a year before. Some memories of being at Brockenhurst and then in the Kaori cemetery at his mother's plot tried to play through in his mind. He resisted though by instead looking at the names of Rita's father and sisters on the wooden plague, which was waiting to be replaced by a permanent headstone. That too was overwhelming so his mind sought distraction. He placed his hand over Rita's hand that was resting on his right forearm to which Rita gently looked up at him. She could see he was preoccupied and now glancing out to a distance. He liked the warmth of the sun upon his face and yet also the freshness of the breeze. He looked down toward the two islands and the bay. He thought it must be high tide again as a large steamer that had been waiting in the stream was now heading to Dunedin.

WATER - 'KOPUTAI'

Wellington, Tuesday, February 3, 1931

In the swiftness of time between the rolling rumble and first jolt John quickly anticipated the ground was about to violently shake. He had felt enough artillery recoil and detonation, ship and train rides, and earthquakes, to know the differences of things approaching underfoot. Stacks of milk cans began to wobble and topple. He stepped away from the falling cans and held on to a column for support while the floor continued to jolt back and forth. When it stopped John looked around and felt thankful that the milk depot had not broken apart. Collin, the depot manager, walked through from the office and asked John if everything was okay and then proceeded to assist John with picking up the cans. John appreciated the offer of help. It had taken him some time to get used to not having Crump around anymore and to be instead working under the city milk department, rather than what had been Crump's own depot. He was also appreciative of having a job, as every day he saw many of his neighbors who were still struggling to find work again. John then realized he had better phone Rita to check on how she and their children were. He was pleased to hear that she was fine too, as was their home. She would check with the schools about their children but felt sure they were all fine too. John assured Rita he would be home as soon as he had finished cleaning up at the depot. Collin then turned on his new radio and searched the tuner for any reports on what had just happened. The local channels were still playing late morning regular items but then Collin came across a short wave broadcast. The speakers of the radio crackled and the small wooden cabinet resonated as the announcer identified himself as Mick Spears. He said he was broadcasting from Blaketown, down on the West Coast of the South Island.

"I am receiving live reports from fellow radio hams right there in Hawke's Bay. The cities of Napier and Hastings have been severely hit! It is feared that many people have been killed"!, voiced Spears with urgency accelerating as he spoke. "Some people killed by falling masonry as they ran out into the streets. Local authorities are saying they think many are trapped under a library and others under a department store. Phone lines are all down. Calling all radio hams to pass on the call to outside authorities for immediate assistance". Spears took a moment's breath then continued. "A report from the HMS Veronica at the Napier wharf has just come through. Captain Morgan is reporting that he saw the stores on the wharf burst asunder and disgorged their bales of wool, railway lines twisted and bent, and the wharf then gave way and fell into the harbor". John and Collin listened intently as Spears continued to read the captain's report. "The city was shrouded in dust. The bed of the sea rose beneath the ship hitting the bottom and the stern wires gave way. The captain thought sure the ship would break her back". Spears then reported on how many people had panicked and had run down to the beaches. Suddenly some realized the water had receded far out from the coast and feared a tsunami might come next and so panicked again and ran for higher ground. But no tsunami has come he said. Spears promised to make more reports as they came in and proceeded to repeat the news received already. Collin then retried a local Wellington channel and heard that announcer report some of the same things of the captain's report, but not much more. At least he and John heard that there were no reports of serious damage or injuries in Wellington. They both looked at the other and without saying anything knew the other's expression meant great relief.

John was satisfied that all had been taken care of at the depot, so hurriedly left to go home to Rita. When he arrived home they both exchanged how shaken they had felt. John filled Rita in on the radio reports he had heard and Rita assured him the school had told her their children were alright. They both felt so sorry for what had happened in the Hawke's Bay. They talked and took stock of all the things they felt thankful for, especially each other and their children. Together they decided to go collect the children when school finished for the day.

By the time the children, Jack and Audrey, arrived home they were still excitedly talking about feeling the earthquake and about how unusual it was for both John and Rita to walk with them from school. Rita put together a few things for an afternoon snack to celebrate their good fortune as a family. Although they had plenty of milk for the children the biscuits were few. Like for many families, the economy was still tough, Rita and John had to ration things very carefully. That included phone calls too, so when Rita's mother phoned before dinner they knew they needed to be brief.

"Oh my dears, I am so glad to hear you are alright. But I feel so sorry for those poor people in Hawke's Bay", said Ellen. "We did not feel anything down here. Anthony phoned to tell me to listen to the radio. It is hard to believe that a hundred or more may have perished. And then also fires too. How terrible! Thank goodness that naval ship was there and the crew were able to go ashore to help".

Rita agreed and then went on to ask after Anthony, her brother, and his wife and son. Ellen said they were all doing well, that little Anthony was a typical two-year old, and that Ruth was expecting again. Ellen then asked about Jack and Audrey. Rita replied they were both doing well at school, Jack at rugby, and Audrey at music and dance.

John sat quietly listening to Rita on the phone. He also heard Jack reiterating to Audrey some of the things about earthquakes he had heard from teachers and from Rita and him too. It reminded him of how Emily, his sister, had taken care to explain things to him when they lived in Christchurch at the time of the 1901 earthquake that had brought down the cathedral spire. He missed Emily, and felt sad he had not seen her since his return from the war and before her passing five years ago. He still struggled with how much time he had lost to exhaustion and confused memories from the war. He wondered what it would have been like for Jack and Audrey to have known his mother and sister.

He felt whole and warm as he thought about how Jack had grown to be considerate of Audrey, Rita and him too. Even while he excelled in sport, Jack was kind in carefully including others who were not as skillful. He would still tease Audrey occasionally, but deep down he was her protector too; just like Emily had been. John sat feeling grateful for his family and the joy they brought him. He felt sure his mother would be smiling as she looked down upon them. She had longed for such full family life. It occurred to him that he had not felt the deep pit inside of himself for some time. He smiled, and, without saying so, Rita saw it and felt warmth bathe her as well.

Wellington, Supreme Court, Monday, December 9, 1935

Rita held her hands up to shield her eyes from the bright sunlight as she looked to locate the aeroplane that was making noise above the city. Her full view of the sky was impeded by the buildings along Lambton Quay, on which she was walking and on her way early to the Supreme Court. The Moth bi-plane came into her field of vision low enough for her to read its ZK-ADP registration and to see that both a pilot and a passenger occupied the two open air cockpits. She walked to the corner of Stout and Whitmore Streets, as did other intrigued pedestrians, in time to see the aeroplane fly over the new railway station still under construction and receiving its tile clad roof. After ascending closer to the few cumulus clouds, hanging around since the overcast weekend, the aeroplane then turned to take a south easterly direction over and away from the harbor. Rita guessed that the pilot must have taken the passenger for bit of a sight-seeing detour over the city because the aeroplane even flew in a direction away from Rongotai aerodrome, which was also south of the city at Lyall Bay. She wondered whether one day Audrey or Jack would get to be passengers in an aeroplane. She imagined it was unlikely she or John would ever take a ride in one.

Once inside the court building Rita found her way to the room she was expected to be at to give her testimony. She remembered the instructions she had been given to remain outside the room, but to be ready as soon as she was called. She sat down on a large wooden pew and discretely looked around at the few other people waiting outside the next room. She did not recognize anyone. The inside atmosphere and pew felt cold to Rita. She was anxious too about having never given testimony before and she hoped to not see Charles Jones or Samuel Williams, whom she suspected would be there as witnesses too. Ordinarily, seeing them at church was fine by her; but the circumstances involving Ethel May had brought some tension for them all. So she tried to distract herself by looking at the large portraits hanging on nearby walls. The paintings were of successive chief justices each standing resplendent in their vestments. One of Queen Victoria, in a large gilded frame, held prominence among them all. Rita thought it strange how there had been a queen but no female justices. She wondered too whether there were any female lawyers. Then she remembered, because of the first name, how Ethel Benjamin had been New Zealand's first woman lawyer.

The sound of other people walking and talking in other corridors echoed down to where Rita sat. She was relieved when those sounds disappeared too, but she still felt anxious sitting alone waiting to be called. She worried about not understanding any questions she might be asked. She hoped to not stammer or say non-sensible things, despite she never had before. Meanwhile she was unaware that the start of the hearing, for which her attendance was soon to be required, was being announced by the bailiff.

"All rise! The Honorable Chief Justice Sir Michael Myers presiding. The plaintiff, Mrs. Ethel May Craigie, represented by messieurs Sievwright and Tripe, is suing the Spiritualist Church of New Zealand and three of its national council for breach of contract and wrongful termination of engagement she had with them to act as a speaker and medium of the church. She also alleges that the defendants wrongfully cancelled her speakers license and her permit to act as a medium. She seeks damages of three hundred pounds. Mr. Treadwell represents the defendant church and Mr. Henry James appears for the three other defendants, Messieurs Samuel Williams, Ernest Gray, and Alfred Heather, president, secretary, and treasurer respectively of the church".

Mr. James stood to cross examine after Sievwright had finished his questioning of Mrs. Craigie to present her case. James knew he too would have to be careful in his approach. He had dealt with Justice Myers before, who had a reputation for being perceptive and demanding of counsel to be succinct. The justice's typical expression was also disconcerting for most counsel. His seemed to always have a piercing stare, while his left cheek and lips were negligibly raised asymmetrically giving the impression he was smirking. The justice was also known for his wit, and he would not disappoint even in this relatively simple case for his court.

James attempted to pose questions to suggest Mrs. Craigie's business was so meager as to be wasting the courts time. Justice Myers was having no such minimization of the case and so asked his own questions to Mrs. Craigie as to her charges for services. She explained,

"I may get as many as twenty people present, and they all pay around two shillings. I had one man recently who paid me five".

"He must have got good news", quipped the justice. Others in the court laughed but quickly resumed their silence.

"As mediums we also have a covenant with the police. We give readings and tell a little of the future. You understand what I mean".

"I don't know that I do".

"Well we predict a little of the future. When your license is granted your name is put into the police. You may be visited by a police woman. Supposing you gave a lot of the future and the police woman did not approve, you would be reported to the national council. You would get a warning, and if you did it again you would go before the court".

"It is fair to say that without a license you run a little more risk than if you had a license"?

"That is quite right, sir. So you see how essential it is to have a license".

Laughter bubbled forth again in the court and erupted even further when Sievwright thought he would try and one-up the justice.

"This is the best advocacy we've had for licensing bookmakers for a very long time".

"I should not like to make that comparison", replied the justice, with others laughing again. Sievwright instead cautiously took it as a slight reprimand and was relieved the change over to a new witness would diffuse the situation for him.

The court room door creaked as it opened. Rita was beckoned inside and directed to the witness stand. She felt her throat go dry and as though it was closing over. The wooden paneling inside made the room feel dark to her and even more foreboding than the halls. Rita again wondered whether she would speak sensibly. She should not have doubted herself as from the outset she gave clear responses as to who she was, where she lived, and her position as secretary of the executive committee for the Wellington branch of the church. She steadied her nerves between questions by studying the ornate moldings in the shape of acorns that adorned the room. Sievwright continued to present the plaintiff's case and asked Rita to verify various things.

"Mrs. Bowen, were you present on Sunday May Fifth this year when Mrs. Craigie was presented her certificate as a medium within the church"?

"Yes, sir. I was there".

" About how many people were present"?

"I would say there were around sixty or so".

"Who presented Mrs. Craigie with her certificate"?

"Mr. Williams".

"What do you recall Mr. Williams said as he gave Mrs. Craigie her certificate"?

"That it would enable her to carry out the duties of speaking from our church's platform, take the meetings as a medium should do, and give private readings".

"What did Mr. Williams say to her about how her duties apply to the national church"?

"He said that her duties would be applicable to our national church and until March of next year".

"Is it correct to say that you, as secretary of the Wellington branch, had already sent Mrs. Craigie a letter outlining how she was engaged in the those duties".

"Yes, I had sent that to her at the knowledge too of Mr. Williams".

"Were you consulted at all by any of messieurs Williams, Gray, or Heather, about terminating any arrangements with or canceling any eligibility of Mrs. Craigie to exercise her duties as a medium or platform speaker in your Wellington church or in the national body"?

"No, sir. I was not asked".

"Is it correct to say that Mrs. Craigie had lost a great deal of income due to having her license withdrawn and her arrangements with the church terminated".

"Yes, sir. I could not say how much but it was probably most of what she depended on from work".

Rita felt relieved when she was dismissed from the witness stand. Instead of leaving the room she sat down at the rear. She was curious to hear other witnesses and the eventual decision on the case by the justice. Treadwell and then James arose to question their witnesses some of whom were also the defendants. Williams could not recall what he had said to Mrs. Craigie at the ceremony in May. All he conceded was that he might have said she would be engaged to provide services through the Wellington branch. He added that the national council had not engaged a medium since 1924, and that engagement was actually through local branches. Rita felt at first embarrassed when Williams explained that he and the other executive members had not included her in their deliberation about Mrs. Craigie due to a letter Rita had written vilifying Mrs. Craigie. Rita then felt instead annoyed that Williams had exaggerated about the letter and she had no way now to explain its content to the justice or Ethel May. It contained nothing more than her observations of Mrs. Craigie being critical of other members, possibly with intent to gain more work for herself, and not unlike other members being sometimes critical of others. Then a Mr. Albert Hastings, from Napier, said he too had been at the national conference in May and had heard Williams' speech when he gave Mrs. Craigie her certificate. Hastings further described that he did not hear Williams say she would be engaged by the national council. He knew of Mrs. Craigie too because she had an arrangement also through the Napier branch, and estimated her weekly earnings had been one pound, thirteen shillings, and five pence per week. To Rita's surprise Justice Myers changed tact on Treadwell's contention that there had been no agreement with the national council.

"I am not bound by that. Suppose there was a contract with a branch, and the corporate body stepped in and prevented it from being carried out"?

"Your Honour, there is no evidence of a contract whatsoever save the offer from Mrs. Bowen on behalf of the Wellington Branch. If any contract was enforceable it would be with the Wellington branch".

"Supposing there was, who prevented the branch from carrying it out"?

"So far as a contract is concerned no one has prevented it from being carried out".

Justice Myers now sounded annoyed. "Yes they did! This executive body chooses to send a letter of August Tenth, which says this lady not only has her licensed cancelled, but she cannot be allowed to go on the platform or be associated with the branch".

"They recommend. It is nothing more than a recommendation".

"It is no use mincing matters on the evidence. The executive did not even have the courage to present here to the court a good reason for having taken away her license and means of livelihood".

"I submit that your Honour is entitled to take a more charitable view as far as the church is concerned. Your Honour need not assume there was no justification".

"Mr. Treadwell, may I point out to you the way in which this thing was done. These three gentlemen met in Christchurch. To some members of the committee, who perhaps they thought might be opposed to what they were doing, they did not give notice. But to the other members, whose approval they are seeking and who are not proposing to attend, they ask for their approval without giving them any reason for the action they are taking; and they don't give this woman, the plaintiff, the opportunity in answering any complaints if there are any or of being heard in any way whatsoever".

"Afterwards, when they invoked rule seventeen to enable her to come and state...".

"After they had done the mischief"!

"After they had done some mischief at any rate". Treadwell was careful not to fully contradict the justice.

"After they had done the whole mischief"! The justice sounded quite irate and showed his disdain by limply banging his gavel to announce he had heard enough and would retire to his chamber to deliberate on his judgment.

Most of the attendees arose from their seats and remained standing as they chatted among themselves. Rita hoped her sense of estrangement from Ethel May, Williams, and all the other church member witnesses would subside soon; but for the time being she elected to stay seated and quiet at the rear of the room. She had brushed off her concerns before about how some church members behave and sometimes toward each other. That is just people being people, she would say to herself. It is their true spirit that counts in the end and they all mean well. But her disappointment in other people had deepened through what she heard this day in the court room. Would she need to find another church, one that John would also attend. It would be a pity to change, it had been a part of her life for a long time. She remembered too the first time she had met Alice, John's mother, at her Spiritualist church. Rita never usually let any doubt linger in her mind but she also began to question whether she had experienced anything through any of the mediums. How she wished she had had some sort of contact from her deceased father or siblings. At least she had pleasant dreams about them and their times together back in Carey's Bay, at school, holidays at home, and waiting and watching for her father's boat to come in. She could, however, never make sense of the recurring dream in which her father would be standing in his boat or at the furthest end of their garden and be frequently saying "Koputai", but nothing else.

"All rise"! The bailiff's loud cry shook Rita from her private reflection. Justice Myers wasted no time in announcing his judgment.

"There has indeed been a breach of contract by the Spiritualist Church, the corporate body. Even if that were not so, the corporate body stepped in and prevented any contract with the local branch from being performed. As to the question of damages, I am satisfied that the damages claimed are excessive. The loss was in my view somewhere between one pound and two pounds a week on the evidence. From August tenth to March Thirty First is just thirty-three weeks, and I think if I allow the sum of fifty pounds by way of damages I shall be doing substantial justice".

Rita fled from the room as soon as the justice had left. She wanted to avoid facing Ethel May or any of the other witnesses. She hoped that an answer to her own deliberations about the church, and the people in it, would present itself sooner rather than later.

Wellington to Carey's Bay, Saturday, October 1, 1938

The speaker cone hidden behind the face of the Philips radio faithfully reproduced a baritone voice that resounded throughout the house. Audrey was anxiously awaiting to hear the 2YA Saturday morning dance program. "Oh, I wish they would hurry up", she said.

"Be quiet Audrey", said her brother Jack, "I want to hear this".

The radio voice continued to announce the sporting events for the weekend, scratchings from the day's horse races, and a reminder of the Sunday scheduled broadcast of the Inter-University debate between Victoria and Otago. Just as the announcements were over Jack played with the tuner dial as though to find another station. The speakers spat out a raspy noise and Audrey voraciously complained to her mother.

"Jack, you leave that radio alone now. You know this is Audrey's time to hear her music", Rita called out from the kitchen." You should go finish packing for your trip".

Audrey was pleased to have the radio and lounge to herself again. At times she would listen intently to the news and the occasional pledge drive. She still felt proud of hearing her name being once announced on 2ZB for her five shilling donation to the King's Memorial Fund. But Saturday mornings were her time to listen and dance to music. As the music flowed from the speakers she began to rise on her feet and to lightly flit her still lithe figure from one end of the room to the other. She imagined herself older and performing for a very appreciative audience some of whom were teachers and examiners from her earlier recitals. As the music changed to a waltz she then imagined a handsome partner flawlessly moving in unison with her and onlookers staring in admiration. Rita looked up from her baking and caught a glance of Audrey sailing through the lounge. She smiled.

Light rain was falling at Carey's Bay so Ellen was indoors too, rather than out in her garden tending for spring flowers and vegetables. She knew Audrey would be doing her Saturday morning dancing and so Ellen had her own radio on Dunedin's 4YA from which dance music flowed through her house too. Ellen looked forward to chatting with Audrey the next occasion on the phone about the music they had each heard and how she was doing with her practice and recitals. She was also excited in anticipation of how her grandson Jack was due to arrive the next day for a holiday with her for the first time on his own. She had consulted with Rita about his likes and dislikes of food. She had dusted off an old bicycle for him to use for whatever adventure about the port he might chose to do alone or with Harry, the local boy Jack had befriended on earlier visits.

Jack was becoming anxious too. He did not want to say so, but he was a little nervous about taking the ferry and train by himself. He put on a brave face though about how he was going to stand out on deck and take in the open sea air. He said he might pay attention to watch the crew, because he was interested in perhaps working on a ship. He did not eat as much as usual at dinner, but Rita chose not to comment. Instead she tucked in some Anzac biscuits into his bag just before hugging him goodbye. Audrey asked him to tell their grandmother she loves her and then also hugged him. John suggested he and Jack had better leave to catch the next tram so as to be on time for the 7.50pm sailing of the Wahine to Lyttleton. John, not one to usually hug his son, when at the wharf grasped Jack's hand to shake but also lay his left arm upon his shoulder.

"You have a good time down there Jack. Oh, and give my best to your grandmother."

John was trying to say he felt proud and hopeful about Jack venturing to travel on his own for the first time. But he could only also say "Once you are at Lyttleton you will do fine at finding the train. There is plenty of ferry staff you can ask about directions. You probably won't need to though". The memory of leaving by ship for the war impeded any further words, but John felt thankful that Jack was instead just going on holiday.

Jack could sense his father wanted to say more and to show his gratitude dropped his bag to also touch his father's shoulder. He thanked his father and then hoisted his bag over his shoulder and made his way on to the ferry. He placed his bag on a seat he thought he preferred and then proceeded out on to the open deck. He watched as the dock and on-board crew prepared for the departure. He then waved to his father whose figure slowly disappeared as the ferry made its way from the wharf and into the harbour. Jack liked the feel of the damp and breezy air against his face. Some of the water droplets lightly stung his skin and caused him to sometimes blink. But he liked the feeling of being out in the open, to watch the ship plow through the water and the waves break against rocks that protruded close to the shore line. The ferry began to toss and lurch a little as it passed through the heads and began the crossing of Cook Straight to travel down the east coast of the South Island. The wind was stronger too and so Jack decided to return indoors for the remainder of the sea journey.

It was late but, unlike other passengers around him, Jack was awake. He was still too excited to sleep. The train continued after its first stop at Timaru and sped down the latter part of the Canterbury plains. It was also dark so Jack could not see much of anything outside except the lights at each station stopped at for brief discharge of a few passengers each time. As the train moved on he could hear the chattering of the wheels change down as he also felt the train begin its gradual climb into the hills of Otago. Jack was at first surprised to hear the sound of the wheels go from chattering to clacking and quickly back again. But he quickly figured out that was happening each time the train had travelled over a river trestle. Just as he was beginning to feel drowsy and ready for sleep he heard the carriage door slam and the conductor call out "Dunedin next stop". The conductor called out again as he got to the other end and then slammed that door behind him too.

Jack knew to look for his uncle and indeed did see him waiting at the center on the very long platform. Anthony greeted him and asked how his trip had been. "We have a bite to eat for you at home, and I bet you are looking forward to a good night's sleep too", said his uncle as he took Jack's bag to carry it for him. Jack followed his uncle through the booking hall and despite his weariness still noted the ornate mosaic floor at his feet and a highly polished balcony above him. Once outside Jack took a few moments to look at the impressive light stone and dark basalt pattern of the station, and the clock tower at its southern end. The soft street lighting added effect to the contrasting features of the station. Anthony gently smiled at recognizing how Jack's awe reminded him of when he was of the same age. He then called for Jack to climb into his Austin Seven car and then drove off with him.

The next morning Jack was awoken by his two younger cousins, Tony and Edward. Their mother Ruth could no longer contain their impatience to see their older cousin and so they eagerly burst into his bedroom. It became impossible to resist their insistence that he arise out of bed and so he went to see their newly acquired toy soldiers. Jack had not noticed what time it was but after a short while his stomach signaled he was in need of breakfast food. Although Ruth, Anthony and the two young cousins had had their breakfast earlier they all still sat with Jack while he ate his. Not much time was wasted after he was finished and off to bathe and get dressed. When he returned from the bedroom he found his four relatives all ready to take him out to the grandmother's at Carey's Bay.

Ellen was so pleased to see Jack. She gave him such a hug that he wondered when she might let go. After showing him the bedroom he would be using the usual offering of tea and biscuits was made with a caveat, to the younger cousins particularly, that lunch was not far off. Tony fended away Edward's insistence that they play with wooden blocks together, like they would often do. Tony wanted to instead stay around Jack, as though Jack somehow had some essence of certitude to share. Jack, however, felt more at ease when after their lunch he felt the focus of attention move away from him. His Uncle Anthony had responded to Ellen's hints about repairs and things needed in and around her house by wandering outside to survey what she meant. Everyone followed suit but before long Jack had unwittingly volunteered to do a short list of odd jobs while there for the week.

After the uncle, aunt and the two young cousins had left to return to Dunedin, Ellen felt pleased to have time alone with Jack. They chatted as she prepared their evening meal and he assisted with peeling potatoes. Ellen gradually came to recognize that some of Jack's mannerisms reminded her of his name-sake Uncle John. She did not remark about this to Jack but quietly savored the warm feeling it gave her. Jack enjoyed the corned beef and white sauce dinner, and slices of Louise cake with a glass of milk for dessert. He jumped up immediately to help when Ellen moved to take dishes back into the kitchen. It took little time for them to wash and dry the dishes and just as they finished it occurred to Ellen to show Jack some family photos. She wanted to him to learn more about his family heritage. To her pleasure Jack took a lot of interest in listening to her tell story after story about his mother as a baby and young girl, his grandfather

Antonio, his Uncle John, and Aunt Norah. Jack started imagining his grandfather going out to sea in his fishing boat, his uncle out rowing in the bay, and of his aunt dressed in school uniform just like girls he knew when he was at school. He wondered what it would have been like to have been around them. Ellen realised after a while that Jack had probably had enough of family history and so offered they could each retire to bed. Jack readily agreed. Ellen decided to herself she could leave playing piano for him until the next day. That will be fun, she thought.

Jack had not yet arisen the next morning when Harry, his friend, arrived to see him. He had been awoken during the night by the sound of hail and later very heavy rain, and so was less eager to get out bed. After a while Ellen decided to go check on Jack and announce that Harry was waiting for him. Once he heard his friend's name Jack did not hesitate to get out of bed and go see him. They were both happy to see each other and together ate the cooked breakfast Ellen had enticed them to stay for. As soon as they had finished eating Jack quickly dressed and returned to the kitchen. Ellen could see his anxiousness to leave but not offend her, and so said she was alright with his going out. Jack said thanks to his grandmother and then headed out the door with Harry and rode off on their bicycles. Ellen felt a little disappointed that Jack had left so early in his visit, but remembered her own sons at the same age were just as impetuous. They would be back as soon as their stomachs signaled hunger. She did not even have time to remind Jack to take his rain coat.

Harry had led Jack down to the wharves at Carey's Bay pressing upon him they had needed to rush. He had remembered Jack's interest in going out on a fishing launch and had gotten them a ride on a neighbor's boat. It was about to go out into the lower harbor to lay nets. Jack felt excitement wash through him as he realized what was being offered. The boat's captain looked a grisly chap though. His first order to the boys to leave their bicycles in a better spot made Jack at first weary about getting on the boat. The captain then beamed a broad smile and said, "I could do with some strong guys as extra help today". Jack felt relieved by the warmer welcome and so jumped on board.

The captain churned the motor over twice before it sputtered and then settled into a low rumbling. Jack could see the water that had been lapping at the boat beginning to be repelled back by the reverberation of the boat. Harry untied the ropes at the captain's request and then jumped on board too. As the boat made its way out of the bay Jack could feel the breeze pick up. He liked the feeling again of the wind flowing against his face and passing through his hair. He momentarily imagined that instead of the captain it was his grandfather at the wheel. How he would have liked to have known him, to have gone out fishing with him. To arrive back home and show what fish they had caught, and the great dinner they would have had together.

The boat proceeded further beyond the protection of the peninsula and out into the main stream. A westerly wind was whipping down from the upper harbor and clamored at starboard as the boat heaved up and down on the choppy waves. The captain steered the launch in behind Goat Island which gave temporary reprieve from the wind and again behind Quarantine Island after withstanding the gusting wind in-between. The launch slowed and stopped at the south end of the larger island. With its motor still idling the captain threw its anchor into the water. Jack did not have to wonder for long about what they would do next. Harry asked Jack to assist him to lower a dinghy over the side. They then each gingerly climbed down into the dinghy while it bobbed around on the choppy water. Jack instinctively found his footing to balance himself and followed Harry's lead to hoist some netting on board with them. They then used their oars to push against and away from the launch. The fishing net gradually unrolled into the water while the dinghy still danced up and over each wave. The captain had instructed Harry to paddle and lay the netting as far as they could across the gap toward the Portobello Peninsula. He hoped to capture many moki or cod from schools that often swam around the southerly side of the harbors.

Harry gave Jack thumbs-up as the signal to turn-about and paddle back to the launch. The wind still gusted down between the island and the peninsula. Jack again liked the sensation of the wind and sea spray on his face, in his hair, and the taste of salt upon his lips. As they began their return he looked to the island and saw that waves were crashing with greater ferocity over outer craggy rocks and on the shoreline. The wind shifted wildly back and forth and the dinghy was lifted higher upon each new wave to slide down again into deeper troughs. Each time they lost sight of the island and the launch the boys became worried, and then more worried. Harry copped a strained smile as though to tell Jack he had things under control. On the next trough the dinghy had trouble rising upward again and instead dug in too deep. The oncoming wave rode over the dinghy and hurled it around as though a piece of drift wood far from which it came and nowhere particularly to go. The boys were discarded into the convulsing water and were thrashed about so much they both lost sense of what was up from down. Harry was the first to find his sense of direction and to make it to the surface. The captain had seen what had happened to the boys and the dinghy and had begun to turn the launch around to head toward them. He could hear Harry calling out Jack's name, again and then again. And then again with even more urgency as Jack came into sight atop of a cresting wave. "This way, Jack! This way Jack"! Harry could see the approaching launch and so made his own way to swim as hard as he could toward it. He hoped Jack had also seen the launch and would swim in the same direction. Jack had indeed seen it and swam as hard as could to move through the heavy swells. With each stroke of his arms he felt the next swell harder and harder to penetrate. He began to feel that he was pushed back by each wave. His clothes began to feel heavy and then heavier. He heard Harry call out his name again. He could hear the fear in Harry's shrill call. He could by now hear the motor of the launch even though he began losing the strength to look up to see how close it might be. His arms began to feel leaden but he still kicked his legs as hard as he could. His legs then too became leaden. He felt his lungs begin to tighten like a vice as he tried to gasp for more air to push through his exhausted body. He could no longer lift his head to take more air. He felt cold and then colder still. His mind began to tell him to just lay down his head as though to take a rest on his own bed. "Perhaps if I just rest a while I might be okay", he thought. He imagined curling up his legs and arms to lie more comfortably. He heard his mother calling him for dinner but he could not get his voice to work to let her know he was on his way. His mind told him to close his eyes to take some sleep. As he did so he felt his bed give way to let him fall into a cold morass below. He suddenly awoke and he held his hands high as though to touch the imaginary sky, in hope Harry, the captain, or his mother and father would see and come grasp his hands. But his lungs filled with water, he struggled to keep his eyes open, and he realized he was losing consciousness.

*

Wellington, Monday, October 14, 1940

Audrey and Ellen were on each side of Rita as they all stood by the hospital bed and as she held John's hand. She had nearly always felt comforted whenever she studied his hands, and had done so many times before. She had seen them age along with John. His hands had softly caressed her, they had cracks and scars from work and the war, and had gently cradled Jack and Audrey when they were babies. She could not now bare to release his hand. He could not now nor ever again lift it and reach out on his own to touch her. He was gone, Rita silently and finally acknowledged to herself. He would not be rising out of bed again every day in the still dark morning hours to deliver his milk. There would be no more cups of tea together. He had so perfected how she liked her tea. In recent months she had seen and heard him in pain as his labored breathing worsened. But still he had made himself go to work each day. Her best friend was a quietly driven man. She recalled the smell on him of the soap he had used to clean his milk cans. It was a smell she fondly savored whenever she had closed her eyes at the sensation of John kissing the nave of her neck. As she stood at his hospital bed she still held his hand and closed her eyes again to try and hold on to more memories; to hold them tight and bright, to not let them recede.

Ellen gently stroked Rita's shoulder and reassured her that John's suffering was over.

That he looked to be in peace. She recalled to herself when she had lost her Antonio. Of the pain she had felt then and how daily things and other people carried her through. She knew to be there daily for Rita and Audrey for now. As she looked at John she thought of how he had been heartbroken over Jack, like she had for her own children. She remembered his heedful stare confirmed her own quiet anguish at their farewell when Anthony departed in June for the new war. She often had wondered what John must have been through and never spoke of from the first war.

Rita had her arm around Audrey. She pulled her in a little tighter when she heard Audrey begin to sob again. Audrey had tried to hold back her tears but memories of her dad flooded her thoughts. She would miss her dad's soothing voice, of catching glimpses of him at dance recitals and school ceremonies, and bringing in fire wood to keep the house warm. She recalled her first and only time of seeing him cry when he heard about Jack. She remembered standing on the hill in Port Chalmers as they laid her brother to rest with her grandfather and the others. She could still see in her mind the broken look of her parents. It was her first time recognizing they were not invincible. And now she had lost her dad too. She gasped again to hold down the feelings up-heaving through her body, but then could not contain them. Her tears streamed down her cheeks and they tasted like salt as they trickled over her lips.

Palmerston North, Wednesday, August 16, 1972

The brakes on Peter's blue Raleigh bicycle screeched as he suddenly came to a halt outside of the second hand store on King Street. He hopped off his bicycle, leaned it against the front of the brick building, and immediately proceeded inside the store. Most of the things on display were much older than his fourteen years of existence but he looked around excitedly to scan the place for objects of his school boy interest. The shop keeper ignored him and instead approached the next entering customer, a woman he thought to be the most likely to have some amount of money in her dangling purse to spend on his meager range of superficially dusted merchandise. That did not bother Peter because he had a mission of a kind in mind. He had already been to other shops and the cobbler's on Albert Street in search of military badges and medals. He did not want the pesky looking shop keeper to interfere with his mission unless he had to be asked about the possibility of things not obviously on display.

Peter's precise purchase specifications were that he would be able to exclaim their uniqueness to any family, friends or visitors who would listen, and be affordable given his ten dollar limit in his pocket. He preferred not to spend his paper round earnings all at once.

In the glass top cabinets in which Peter expected to see some gleaming badges and medals, there were none. There were instead, disappointingly, gaudy broaches, rings and necklaces that to Peter were reminders of old aunts having tea with their pinkies out while dissecting family goings-on they actually had little knowledge of. No one family member seemed safe from their ill-disguised sympathy, particularly if anyone had spurned attendance to the gathering at hand. Thank goodness, he remembered, that the ginger squares or lamingtons were sufficient bounty to stuff his boredom with sweet distractions. Food, more precisely desserts, was what could contain him in a room of visiting relatives just long enough before busting out to venture outdoors or in his own imagination with special belongings he brought on every trip. It was as a youngster that satisfaction with food and fascination with collecting became his modus operandi. The enjoyment of finding silver three pence or six pence coins in hot fruit pudding, dolloped with whipped cream, had been a highlight for him at Christmas. It was not just the face value of the coins that intrigued him, but also the royal heads or other iconic features too. Collecting coins and then stamps eventually burgeoned into also collecting military badges and medals. It had not yet occurred to him that having been taken around to antique shops and to family reunions by his mother that an interest in preserving history had probably rubbed off on him. For now he handled his collections with fantasies of being himself heroic in great battles of past world wars and of those in his future.

The shop keeper's enquiry interrupted Peter's day-dreaming.

"What are you looking for son?"

"Um, for badges. I did not see any out here. Do you have anything out back?"

"If you mean military badges and things, then no. But I do have this over there on the wall."

Peter had been so preoccupied with finding badges or medals he had not seen the war service certificate hanging near the front door. He began to study its ornate print of a soldier standing by Britannia, with lions and a slain eagle at her feet, battleships in the background, and Maori motives as side notes to a crown. His excitement began to wane when he saw it had a slight rip.

"How much is it? It does have a rip in it."

"Twelve, but you can have it for ten".

Peter surprised himself by immediately saying he would take it, then stepped back to question himself again about spending all his money. The shop keeper sensed Peter's hesitancy.

"It is a great piece of war history. It came in just last week from over on Fitzroy Street. No one else to take the lady's stuff. This certificate was probably her father's".

"I live just around the corner".

"Maybe you knew her. Number forty two, Miss Audrey Bowen".

Peter thought for a moment, shook his head, then quickly went back to thinking about what battles the man might have been in. The shop keeper wrapped the certificate in old newspaper and handed it to Peter.

When nearly home he decided to take a ride on Fitzroy Street. Forty-two was not part of his paper route so he was curious to see the house. He dared to ride partly down the drive to get a better look at forty-two, but nothing distinguished it from forty-four at front. Both were small plain looking cement block single dwellings.

"Did you know her"? A voice from behind Peter caught him by surprise.

"Um…". Peter did not know what to say. He glanced down at the package with the certificate. "No, not really".

"I was paying my own respects. I grew up in the house over the back fence".

The man seemed almost robotic and his eyes had a haunting glaze, but he spoke again.

"Ms. Audrey was a nice lady, was kind to all us kids around here".

Peter felt relieved when the man walked away and did not question him further.

But there was something about the man's headband and camouflage jacket that struck Peter as being unusual. Then it dawned on him, but he did not have the gumption to ride and catch up to the man and ask if he had been in Vietnam.

EPILOGUE

IN MEMORIAM
BOWEN.-In loving memory of my husband,
John Frederick, 11-402, who passed away
October 14, 1940. Also my dear son, John
Cabral Bowen, accidentally drowned
October 3, 1938.
>Fondly remembered.
>By Mum and Audrey.

[Evening Post, Volume CXXXII, Issue 91, 14
October 1941, page 1].

N.Z. ROLL OF HONOUR
DEATHS

CABRAL. – Private Anthony Cabral, killed in
action, dearly-beloved husband of Ruth
Cabral, 385 King Edward Street, Dunedin,
and brother of Mrs. R. Bowen, 133 Wallace
Street, Wellington. R.I.P.

[Evening Post, Volume CXXXII, Issue 139, 9
December 1941, page 1].

CABRAL ELLEN 73 Years Female Date of
Death
30 Dec 1943. PORT CHALMERS CEMETERY
Block SB. Plot 115. Burials also in this Plot:
CABRAL HILDA 2 Years, Died 13 Aug 1914

CABRAL ANTONIO 48 Years, Died 24 Apr
1916
CABRAL NORAH 13 Years, Died 17 Jun 1918
CABRAL JOHN 19 Years, Died 18 Feb 1920
BOWEN JOHN CABRAL 19 Years, Died 3 Oct
1938

[www.dunedin.govt.nz/facilities/cemeteries
/cemeteries_search]

BOWEN, AUDREY JOSEPHINE Female,
SPINSTER, 42 FITROY STREET,
Denomination not known, 49Y Date of Death
02/06/1972, Place of Death unknown
Date of Internment 06/06/1972 Kelvin
Grove Cemetery
Area J Block 013 Plot 094
Funeral Director THOMAS GRIGGS & SON
LTD
Book of Memories NO

[www.pncc.govt.nz/services/onlineservices
/cemetery-and-cremation search].

[NOTE: have not been able to find records on
births, death, or marriages for Emily Bowen
(John Frederick's sister) or for Rita's death
(John Frederick's wife)].

SUPPORTING NOTES TO CHAPTERS

Palmerston North, New Zealand, Thursday, June 1, 1972

The record at
www.pncc.govt.nz/services/onlineservices/cemete
ry-and-cremation search lists
Audrey as having died as a spinster. I could find no
other information about her as an adult and how
she ended up in Palmerston North. So this first
chapter is partially based upon information about
her and her family when she was a child.

Christchurch, New Zealand, Saturday, September 2, 1893

This chapter is mostly fictional but places the main
true characters of Alice, Emily, John, and Charles
who lived in Christchurch in a context for their
time; with women's right to vote first occurring in
New Zealand (NZ); and how Kate Sheppard,
suffragette of the Women's Christian Temperance
Union (NZ), came from Christchurch, NZ. It
coincided that Ernest Rutherford had in
Christchurch begun his study of nuclear physics.

Christchurch Supreme Court, Monday, August 17, 1896

True events as recorded previously in:

A PECULIAR CASE. THE CUSTODY OF A CHILD.
The Star, Issue 5593, 17 June 1896, page 3

SUPREME COURT. Criminal Sittings.
The Star, Issue 5646, 18 August 1896, Page 3
(The above and following newspaper references were found via paperspast.natlib.govt.nz).

Christchurch, Saturday, May 4, 1907

This chapter is also mostly fictional but places Emily and John in a context of changes and events in and around Christchurch at that time. The story 'The Man From Temuka' represents the 31 March 1903 test flight by Richard Pearce. 'The Seaside Sentry', made up for this book, represents how Ngaio Marsh, a famous NZ author, grew up in the Christchurch area.

Christchurch Magistrates Court, Tuesday, May 7, 1907

True events as recorded previously in:

A CHARGE OF ASSAULT: A Precious Document, The Star, Issue 8922, 7 May 1907, Page 3.

Wellington, New Zealand, Thursday, October 28, 1915

Based closely on John Frederick Bowen's (Serial No. 11402) enlistment records which were available through: www.archway.archives.govt.nz/ViewFullItem.do?code=22277809 and *muse.aucklandmuseum.com/databases/Cenotaph/ AdvancedSearch*

W Crump's dairy of Rintoul Street, Berhampore, amalgamated with other milk companies to form The Nutricia Milk Company of (Cornhill Street) Wellington, Sept 30 1911.

Trentham, New Zealand, Sunday, April 23, 1916

John's records indicate he did his training at the Trentham military camp, not the camp at Featherston.

Petone, New Zealand, ANZAC Anniversary, Tuesday, April 25, 1916

There was no direct evidence of John having attended the first anniversary ANZAC ceremony at Petone. However, I included him in this context to convey what it might have been like for a newly enlisted soldier hearing about the war before his own departure. This chapter also conveys the political attitudes of the time' of how New Zealand

and Australia were still seen as post-colonial dominions of Great Britain. However, the feeling of being badly used by the British in the first stages of World War One inspired some talk of seeking independence. Yet it took many more decades to begin true bi-cultural independence.

ANZAC DAY, DOMINION, Vol. 9, Issue 2752, 22 April 1916, page 6.
ANZAC DAY at Petone, Evening Post, Vol. XCI, Issue 95, 22 April 1916, page 6.
N.S.W. and N.Z. Railwaymen Ceremony at Petone Evening Post, Vol. XCI, Issue 98, 26 April 1916, page 2.
The Ceremony at Hornsby, Evening Post, Vol. XCI, Issue 98, 26 April 1916, page 2.
Photo: Petone Flagpole ANZAC Day 1916:
http://www.150yearsrail.org.nz/petone-flagpole-anzac-day-service-unique-in-honouring-railway-fallen].

Wellington to Egypt, Monday, May 1, 1916

John's actual role in movements and actions with his battalion were not detailed in his military service records. So the following references were used to recreate the context based on date periods in which he was actively serving.

Burton, O.E., The Auckland Regiment: being an account of the doings on active service in the First, Second and Third Battalions of the Auckland Regiment. Whitcomb and Tombs, Auckland, 1922;

http://nzetc.victoria.ac.nz/tm/scholarly/tei-WH1Auck.html

Butler, S., New Zealand Mounted Rifles: The Mackesy Family, March 2006; http://www.nzmr.org/mackesy.htm

McFadgen, A., Private William Arthur Ham, The Prow.org.NZ, 2012/2013, http://www.theprow.org.nz/yourstory/private-william-arthur-ham/#.U-JQi6N5mSN.

(Willie Ham, age 22, first NZ death of WW I , injured on Feb 5 1915 battle at Ismailia, Egypt, Suez Canal, died Feb 7th; from Ngatimoti, near Nelson).

Stewart, H., Col.,The New Zealand Division 1916 - 1919: A Popular History Based On Official Records. Whitcombe and Tombs, Auckland, 1921. New Zealand Electronic Text Collection: http://nzetc.victoria.ac.nz/tm/scholarly/tei-WH1-Fran.html
-pg 609 on the numbers of New Zealand troops and nurses who served in the war was around 110,000 out of a population of slightly over one million only.

Weston, C.H., Lt. - Col., Three Years With The New Zealanders, Sheffington and Son, Ltd., London, 1918; http://net.lib.byu.edu/estu/wwi/memoir/NZ/kiwiTC.htm

Sling Camp, Bulford, England, Sunday, August 13, 1916

Based on a letter by Alister Robinson to his parents and Nancy June 11 1916, found on NZine, listed March 23 2001; and notes by an unknown Kiwi soldier listed on RootsWeb by Paul Darrall, Hamilton, Oct 5 2002.

The Somme, France, Saturday, September 30, 1916

Based again upon Burton (1922), Stewart (1921), and Weston (1918).

NZ Division in action Sept 15 1916 where British tanks used first time at village of Flers, near Longueval; Battle of Flers- Courcelette.

New Zealand Field Hospital, France, Wednesday, October 18, 1916

Based on John Frederick Bowen's (Serial No. 11402) military records which showed dates of injury and places treated. www.archway.archives.govt.nz/ViewFullItem.do?code=22277809.

Neuve Eglise, Belguim, Sunday, May 6, 1917

Based again upon Burton (1922), Stewart (1921), and Weston (1918).

New Zealand General Hospital, Brockenhurst,
England, Tuesday, July 10, 1917

Based again on John Frederick Bowen's (Serial No.
11402) military records which showed dates of
injury and places treated.
www.archway.archives.govt.nz/ViewFullItem.do?c
ode=22277809.

Maclean, H., Nursing in New Zealand: History and
Reminiscences, Tolan Printing Company, 1932;
http://nzetc.victoria.ac.nz//tm/scholarly/tei-
MacNurs-t1-body-d38.html

The Marquette Angels - 23rd October 1915 -
Aegean Sea,
http://www.rootsweb.ancestry.com/~nzlscant/ma
rquette.htm

Treanor, K., Capt., The No. 1 NZ General Hospital
(Brockenhurst) Staff List, complied for Southern
Life, UK, by Capt. Treanor, curator of the Royal New
Zealand Army Medical Corps Museum;
http://southernlife.org.UK/nzstaff.htm

Kaori, Wellington, New Zealand, Thursday,
November 28, 1918

Germany Out Of The War, The Armistice Signed,
Evening Post, Vol. XCVI, Issue 116, 12 November
1918, page 7.
Deaths, Evening Post, Vol. XCVI, Issue 127, 25
November 1918, page 1.

Deaths, Evening Post, Vol. XCVI, Issue 128, 26 November 1918, page 1.
'The 1918 flu pandemic',
http://www.nzhistory.net.nz/culture/influenza-pandemic-1918,
Ministry for Culture and Heritage, updated 3 December 2013.

Francis, N., Tui, in New Zealand Mounted Rifles: Trooper Hugh Gordon Haswell;
http://www.nzmr.org/haswell.htm.

World War One Campaigns of the New Zealand Mounted Rifles: Actions in Gallipoli – Sinai - Palestine;
http://www.nzmr.org/campaigns.htm.

Wellington, Tuesday, January 28, 1919

Alice's association with the Spiritualist Church was referenced in:
A CHARGE OF ASSAULT: A Precious Document, The Star, Issue 8922, 7 May 1907, Page 3.
While Rita's association, possibly via Alice, was referenced in:
A Church At Law: Spiritualist Case: A Medium's Claim Predicting The Future. Evening Post, Volume CXX, Issue 138, 7 December 1935, page 15.

Cabral, Antonio FL 1913: Certificate of Naturalization. Ref: MS - Papers - 5838 – Alexander Turnbull Library, Wellington, New Zealand.
http://natlib.govt.nz/records/22863754?search%5Bpath%5D=items&search%5Btext%5D=Cabral.

H.M. Chapman- Cohen, Koputai (The Very High Tide), in The New Zealand Railways Magazine, Volume 14, Issue 6 (September 1939), New Zealand Government Railways Department, Wellington. Via New Zealand Electronic Text Collection, Victoria University of Wellington; http://nzetc.victoria.ac.nz/tm/scholarly/tei-Gov14_06Rail-t1-body-d12.html.

Port Otago Next Generation Channel Development - Short History of Otago Harbour Development and Dredging, Port Otago, Ltd., 9 June 2009; http://www.portotago.co.nz/publications/15%20S hort%20History%20of%20Harbour%20Dredging %20(Davis%202009).pdf.

St. Joseph's Convent, Port Chalmers New Zealand Tablet, Volume XXXVII, Issue 1, 7 January 1909, page 17.

Carey's Bay, Port Chalmers, New Zealand, Saturday, January 31, 1920

Advertisement Column 2: Funeral Notices, Otago Daily Times, Issue 17864, 20 Feb 1920, page 4.
Deaths, Otago Daily Times, Issue 17861, 17 Feb 1920, page 4.
News In Brief, Otago Daily Times, Issue 17861, 17 February 1920, page 10.
Port Chalmers Hospital Opening Ceremony Otago Daily Times, Issue 15057, 2 February 1911, page 4.

Rowing, Otago Daily Times, Issue 17850, 4
February 1920, page 8.
Rowing: Dunedin Regatta Otago Daily Times, Issue
17847, 31 January 1920, page 6.
Rowing: Dunedin Regatta Successful Revival Otago
Daily Times, Issue 17859, 14 February 1920, page
15.
Rowing: Otago Rowing Association, Otago Daily
Times, Issue 18043, 17 September 1920, page 6.
St. Clair Drowning Fatality, Otago Daily Times, Issue
17861, 17 Feb 1920, page 3.

Wellington, Tuesday, February 3, 1931

City of Napier, Civil Defence and Emergency:
Previous Incidents, 1931 Earthquake;
http://www.napier.govt.nz/services/civil-defence-
emergency/previous-incidents/napier-earthquake-
1931/.

Kling, W., The Municipal Milk Plant of Wellington,
New Zealand., Journal of Farm Economics, Vol. 21,
No. 3, Part 1 (August 1939), pp. 665-668.
http://www.jstor.org/stable/1232151.

Radio NZ audio player 2457192, Jack Perkins,
Napier Quake Anniversary, 2011

Wellington City Milk- supply Act 1919, Early New
Zealand Statutes, University of Auckland Library,
http://www.enzs.auckland.ac.nz/document/?wid=
3771.
Wellington City Milk- supply Amendment Act 1926;
Early New Zealand Statutes, University of Auckland

Library,
http://www.enzs.auckland.ac.nz/docs/1926/1926
L004.pdf.

Supreme Court, Wellington,Monday, December 9,
1935

True events as recorded previously in:
A Church At Law: Spiritualist Case: A Medium's
Claim Predicting The Future. Evening Post, Volume
CXX, Issue 138, 7 December 1935, page 15.

A Church Sued: Spiritualist Case Claims For
Damages, Medium's Engagement. Evening Post,
Volume CXX, Issue 139, 9 December 1935, page 11.

Successful Claim: Medium Awarded Fifty Pounds,
Spiritualist Case A Breach Of Contract. Evening
Post, Volume CXX, Issue 140, 10 December 1935,
page 14.

Michael Myers (judge):
en.m.wikipedia.org/wiki/Michael_Myers_(judge)

Wellington to Carey's Bay, Saturday, October
1,1938

Deaths, Evening Post, Vol CXXVI, Issue 82, 4 October
1938, page 1.
Fishing Tragedy: Youth Drowned Resident of
Wellington, Evening Post, Volume CXXVI, 4 October
1938, page 18.

King George V Memorial Fund: The Mayor's List
Evening Post, Volume CXXIII, Issue 119, 21 May
1937.
Sailor's Society Evening Post, Volume CXXII, Issue
143, 14 December 1936, page 3.
Shipping News: Departures Saturday, October 1,
Evening Post, Volume CXXVI, Issue 81, 3 October
1938, page 12.
The Eisteddfod: Today's Judging: Dancing and
Elocution Evening Post, Volume CXXI, Issue 117, 19
May 1936.

Wellington, Monday, October 14, 1940

Deaths, Evening Post, Volume CXXX, Issue 92, 15
October 1940, page 1.
Funeral Notices, Evening Post, Volume CXXX, Issue
92, 15 October, page 1.
In Memoriam: Bowen, Evening Post, Volume
CXXXII, Issue 91,14 October 1941, page 1.

Palmerston North, Wednesday, August 16, 1972

Mostly fictional but depicts how the World War One
Service Certificate was actually purchased by 'Peter'
not long after Audrey Bowen died in June 1972. The
certificate was loaned to the Featherston Heritage
Complex in Jan 2014 in time for anniversary
displays of World War One. It would be very
pleasing if any descendant of John Bowen's did
make contact with the author or Featherston
Heritage Complex so the certificate can be returned
to his family.

ACKNOWLEDGMENT

I want to acknowledge my wife Karen and my friends Jude, Bill, Eileen and Ed, for their editorial suggestions for improving my writing of this story.

www.ingramcontent.com/pod-product-compliance
Lightning Source LLC
Chambersburg PA
CBHW070750180626
46818CB00007B/3060